DARKNESS

Terence West

DARKNESS

DOUBLE DRAGON

Dedication

To my daughter Lexi:
May your life be wonderful and rich and all your
dreams fulfilled.

PART ONE

One Soul…

It will not be easy.

It will be a life without reward, without remorse, without regret.

This path is placed before you, stretching out endlessly into the horizon. The road forks and winds into countless millions of different possibilities, each changing everything.

But the path is yours alone.

It will not be easy.

PROLOGUE

White fog laced with heavy black smoke from the numerous campfires drifted over what would become the night's battlefield. As the last rays of sunlight began to sink in a pink and orange haze behind the horizon, the far-off sound of inhuman war cries began to waft over the peaceful grassy plain. To the east sat a dense line of trees that cut like a scar across the pristine green field before them. Darkness, even in midday, seemed to cling to this place as if it were a mother protecting its young. It swooped in and around the grizzled branches of the trees and vegetation, providing a soupy blanket that most sane men would not penetrate.

On this night, they had no choice.

It was the year 1704 of their lord, a day when all must be sacrificed for the good of mankind. The encroaching darkness had moved too far into the world of man. They vowed to draw the line here and no farther. These creatures were more like a plague than an invading army. They would attack with sheer animal ferocity, all the while, harvesting the dead soldiers to their own ranks. To send wave after wave of soldiers at them did nothing more than bolster their army, yet this was what the Esgobaeth had seen. This was the way it must be.

Many did not see the wisdom of the Esgobaeth—the High Council—yet Solomon Cole was beginning to. The upcoming battle, while important to the men here today, held significance for the future, no matter the outcome. Tonight would be a defining moment for the Gwyliad Wriaeth. Cole was starting to understand that. Sir Solomon Cole was a knight of the British Empire. He fought for those in the realm who could not do so. This was his sworn duty and he would die to uphold it. It was this belief in duty and honor that led him to the White Guard. Swathed in mystery and disinformation, they were fighting a war they went to great lengths to conceal from all prying eyes. There was greater importance here than the empire's acquisition of wealth and land. These men were defending the future. Cole could not let this call go unheeded. He was fighting tonight for the very fate of every man, woman, and child on Earth.

Drawing his broad sword from its sheath, Cole listened to the clink of his plate armor as he gripped the hilt with both hands. Clad from head to toe in meticulously crafted armor and chain mail, he sat proudly on the back of his sturdy, powerful steed. A bloody, jagged wound sliced from his left cheek to his throat, spilling blood on the silver and gold breastplate of his armor—a trophy from the previous night's engagement. His mocha colored hair fell down from his head in curly waves and terminated just above the imperial purple collar of his shirt. His dark brown eyes scanned the empty battlefield ahead as the sounds of war once again met his ears.

The armored segments on his gloves scraped together as he moved the sword into one hand and lifted it high above his head. Turning to look behind him, he surveyed his men. Each clad in various bits of armor and common clothing, they held their weapons at the ready. Hands shook and lips trembled as they faced what they knew would probably be their final moonrise. Some were extremely young, having just entered Her Majesty's Service, while others had weathered far too many winters. Yet, each was willing to fight and die at Cole's side, no questions asked.

A proud smile flickered across Cole's face as he pulled on his horse's reins and turned the beast toward the men. "You men should all be commended on your courage," he boomed. "You are not fighting for the queen or England, but rather, for the lives of our children, and our children's children." He began to pace back and forth in front of his regiment. "I do not know what the future holds for us," he admitted, giving the men a brief glimpse of the same fear that ran cold through their veins, "but tonight, mankind takes back the night!"

The men cheered loudly.

"Tonight," Cole paused, "we fight!"

Wild cheers erupted among the men as they clanged their weapons together and stamped their feet. Turning back to the battlefield, Cole saw the first of the golden-eyed demons break free of the trees. Taking a deep breath, he gripped his horse's reins tightly in his armored hand. Pointing his sword forward, he dug his spurred heels into the horse sending it surging ahead.

"Charge!"

As Cole's army of Wraiths raced across the green field, they caught the first glimpse of their enemy. Looking like nothing more than fragile, gray, reanimated corpses, each creature's eyes burned a shimmering gold that illuminated the night. As the creatures spilled from the eternal darkness of the forest onto the battlefield, the men quickly spotted a few who had previously been among their ranks. Several of the creatures wore shattered bits of armor and shreds of white fabric— the traditional color of the Wraith. To Cole's horror, the demons began to change. Their demonic forms melted away in favor of healthy pink flesh and clothes that were not previously there. They quickly began to mimic the appearance of Cole's army. Cursing under his breath, Cole locked his eyes onto one of the men he knew was an enemy and pushed his horse faster toward the fray.

As the battle was joined, a fallen horse's scream shattered the cool evening air. The creatures surged ahead into Cole's ranks, clawing and destroying as they went. Moving almost too fast for the human eye, the first wave tore through the Wraiths with pure, animal ferocity. Men were ripped from their mounts and flung across the battlefield like children's toys, while others never had the chance to strike. It was as if a dark tide washed into the army and sent them sprawling helplessly across the ground.

Several of Cole's men fought ahead undaunted, their silver blades carving a swath through the darkness. As a man was picked off from behind, Sir Gerard, one of the few of Cole's fellow knights to join the Gwyliad Wriaeth, lifted a fallen banner from the ground. Holding it high as he cut and slashed, he forged ahead, even though his horse had

12

been killed. Five men followed Gerard's lead and fought brilliantly through wave after wave of oncoming demons. However, luck was not on their side this night. One by one, the creatures dismantled the unit.

Holding the banner in his left hand, Gerard struck ahead with his sword, embedding the blade deep in the heart of a golden-eyed soldier, now more determined than ever. Snapping his gaze to the right, he saw three pairs of gold eyes materialize out of the darkness. Ripping his sword free of the demon, he spun on his toes just in time to cut down the first and second attacker. The third leapt over the bodies of the other two and came crashing down onto Gerard's chest. The knight let out a grunt of pain as the breastplate crumpled into his ribs under the force of the blow. Focusing his eyes on the creature pinning him in place, he could see nothing but the glistening, pearl-white fangs. Mustering every bit of saliva left in his mouth, Gerard spit at the creature's face. "I die for the glory of Her Majesty."

The creature sneered, "You think so?"

Snapping Gerard's head to the side, the creature lunged for his throat. Gerard gnashed his teeth together as the creature's fangs broke through the flesh of his neck.

Slashing down with his sword, Cole easily lopped the head from his first target. Bright blue flame surged from the creature's body as it writhed on the ground in agony. Slowly, red embers began to flit into the air as its body was reduced to ash. Snapping his head around, Cole struck again and

13

again. As an unholy blue fire blazed around him, he lifted his sword high into the air. "Death to all vampires!" he roared.

Turning, he saw his men falling quickly to the advances of the vampire army. Rage gripped him. This was not a battle they were destined to win. The vampire's numbers were far too great. The Esgobaeth had sent them carelessly to their deaths. All his men would be sacrificed on this field. For what cause, for what future purpose would this serve? Hundreds would die here tonight. Gritting his teeth, Cole decided, at that moment, he would not be one of them. He would fight until there were no vampires left standing. Spinning around, he charged blindly into the waves, killing everything he saw.

As the last remaining soldiers under his command fell, he found himself surrounded on all sides by leering golden eyes. His steed whinnied and bucked, almost knocking him free of his saddle. He held on tightly knowing that the horse was his only advantage. The wave of darkness surged forward again, ripping and tearing at him. His steed whinnied and bucked again and again as it tried to escape the claws and fangs, but it was no use. There were simply too many of them. As his horse was brought down, Cole continued to fight, slashing wildly with his sword. The screams of his men filled his ears as his mount came down hard, pinning his right leg beneath it.

"The Wraith will never give up," he grunted in pain. "I promise you!"

The scores of golden eyes hovered around him

in the inky darkness, hissing and giggling with glee. In one horrible movement, they surged toward Cole. He flailed wildly as the razor-sharp claws and fangs dug into his exposed flesh. Piece by piece, his armor was ripped away, exposing the clothing and flesh beneath. He roared in rage as the claws of unseen bodies began to tear at the golden crest of his family emblazoned on the purple shirt he wore. As the claws ripped through his shirt, he lifted his eyes toward the heavens. Blocking out the pain, he uttered a silent prayer in the hopes that God would look after his wife and child. He screamed in agony as the first set of fangs dug into his flesh.

CHAPTER ONE

The room was bathed in darkness as the hopefuls were led inside. These were the chosen few, those who had completed the training and excelled in their courses. This would be part of their final test. If they passed, they would continue the crusade begun centuries ago; if they failed, it meant certain death. Such as it had been for hundreds of years, so would it continue to be with this new generation. As the hopefuls were led through the darkness, each was instructed to kneel with their hands clasped behind their backs. If they were to break the link of their hands at any time, this test would become null and they would lose their chance to complete the training. There would be no make-up day if they failed, no do-overs. This portion of the test was far too important.

Each of the seven—the largest graduating class the academy had seen in some time—were blindfolded to keep them from seeing the members of the High Council. This was done for not only the student's safety, but also for the council members. Though it was not revealed at any point in the training, as a Wraith aged, their features became more and more vampiric in nature. It was becoming increasingly difficult to differentiate between actual vampires and the oldest members of the order. It was also required to keep the student from knowing which member of the council had chosen them for the ritual. Each member of the High Council, or Esgobaeth, was well over one thousand years old, but there were a few older and their "gift" varied according to age. If students had their choice, it was common knowledge they would always chose the eldest member of the council to complete the ritual; however, they knew that not all students could handle, or were worthy of, that much power to begin their careers. The seven watched each member of a class closely, determining whom they would pick for the ritual.

The seven students were all men, save for one woman. A female Wraith wasn't as uncommon as it used to be; yet the council found that few actually completed the training. They were all nearly the same age of twenty-five, with a few a little younger. The female student, Emily St. Louise— her peers called her Saint—was the youngest at twenty-three. She had been observed with special interest by the council for exhibiting a special aptitude for this kind of work. Handpicked for the academy by her Master, Ben Quinn, at the ripe young age of thirteen, she had instantly excelled at her studies and fieldwork. This was rare in a student. Many took months, even years to adjust to their new way of life, while others could not cope at all and washed out. The council had been very impressed with her work over the past ten years and subsequently had chosen her to receive the ritual from the eldest among them: One.

As a Wraith ascended to the council—a spot was rarely ever available—they lost their name and individual identity. Each was given only a number to cling to, the order in which they joined the council. To keep personal wants and needs out of the master equation, these were stripped from a new

17

member. They would think only of the Gwyliad Wriaeth. Nothing else mattered to them anymore. If any of their number began to show personal interest in matters outside the order, the remaining six members dealt them with quickly. This had only happened once in the history of the Guard, but even hundreds of years later, the ripple of consequence was still being felt. It would not be allowed to happen again.

As the two attending Wraiths completed situating the students and informing them of the rules of the ritual, they stepped out of the way and faded into the darkness. The students could hear the slight rustle of fabric as the silence closed in around them. From the head of the immense room, the seven council members appeared as hundreds of candles flickered brightly around them. Each one, dressed in a long, white robe that hid their gender and shadowed their faces, held a ceremonial cup and dagger. Though they were all old enough to have developed fangs, to use them would be an affront to everything they stood for. It would make them no better than the prey they swore their lives to hunt and destroy.

The first—One—stepped out of line and moved in front of the other six council members. Holding the silver dagger in its hand, it pointed to the students. "On this twenty-eighth day of October, in the year two-thousand and four, we are gathered here to transform these students into Acolytes." Its voice was full and deep as it echoed off the cavernous walls of the council chamber. "If there is one here who wishes to refuse the ritual, let

18

them speak now." One paused, although it knew none would speak out. "Very good," it said with more than a hint of pleasure in its voice.

One motioned to the other members of the council to take their positions. As each moved across the room, a row of candles shimmered to life as they walked, lighting their way. Stopping in front of their chosen student, the candles encircled the two, separating each pair from the others. Setting the cups before the students, the council members knelt down and held their daggers at the ready.

"If you scream out," One warned, "you will fail this test. If you unclasp your hands, you will fail this test. If you touch any of the council in any way, you will fail this test." One looked to the other council members, then back to the young woman kneeling before it. "This ritual has been passed down through the generations. It will be the penultimate test in your training, and though you have made it this far, know that this ritual is not without its dangers. I give each of you one final chance to back out and spare yourselves what could be a horrible death."

Again, no one spoke.

"Let the ritual begin."

Moving its hand carefully, One wrapped its fingers around Saint's neck. Tilting her head back, it could feel her heart throbbing in the veins of her throat. It was fear that gripped her, yet she was doing her best to remain strong. Lifting the dagger up, the ancient Wraith pressed it to the side of her throat. With one swift stroke, it pulled the blade through the soft, pink flesh, splaying it open. Blood instantly spurted from the wound as an artery was cleaved in two. Without a single grunt or wince of pain, Saint began to bleed to death. Pushing her head down, One watched her crimson life spill over the hard stone floor around them. Turning to its right, One could see the process repeated on each of the students. To One's approval, none cried out at the quick flash of steel.

Holding its fingers firmly on Saint's throat, it could feel her heart beginning to slow. From its own experience, One knew she was very near slipping from consciousness. The ritual had to be timed precisely. This was the reason ancients only completed it. If they didn't wait long enough, the ritual wouldn't take and the student would be lost, yet if they waited too long, the student would die. It was a fine line they treaded, nevertheless, each was confident in their abilities. Lifting Saint back into a kneeling position, One steadied her with its hands as blood rolled down onto its white robe. "Hold on, my child," it whispered. "It's only just begun." Lifting the dagger again, One pressed it firmly to its own wrist. Pulling once, it laid open its veins. Setting the blade aside, it quickly reached for the cup.

As One held its wrist over the cup quickly filling it, Saint began to feel herself slipping away. Darkness encroached over her brain, threatening at any moment to sever her connection to this reality. The gaping wound in her neck throbbed with pain with every heartbeat, every breath. No longer could she feel her arms and legs, the pain was all-consuming. Reaching down deep into herself, she summoned a strength she had only glimpsed before. She had to hold on. To come so far in ten years, only to die on the council chamber floor would not only disgrace the order, but herself as well. She would not fail, not this close to the finish.

One lifted the cup of its own blood with two hands toward Saint. Its hands trembled slightly, but it quickly calmed itself. To lose this student now would be a tragedy, but fate always had its own agenda. Tipping the young woman's head back, One began to pour the blood into her mouth. Saint gagged as the thick, lukewarm substance hit the back of her throat. One held his hand firmly around her mouth refusing to let her spit any out. She needed every drop to complete the ritual. "Swallow, child," One said, almost pleadingly. "Swallow."

Saint's eyes rolled back as she choked on the liquid. Pulling a breath in through her nose, she closed her mouth and opened her throat. Gulping down the thick substance, her eyes opened wide, then snapped shut. It felt like battery acid chewing its way down her throat. She felt the immediate urge to retch, but clenching her teeth, she fought it. Balling up her fists behind her back, she felt the blood hit her stomach like a brick. Doubling over in pain, she narrowly missed One with her head as she hit the floor. Making sure to keep her hands clasped behind her back, she rested her forehead on the floor amidst a pool of her own blood. Gritting her teeth, she wanted to cry out, but refused. She felt as if red hot needles were being pushed into her skin and muscles over and over again. Intense pain rocketed through her skull as her upper canine teeth were broken and forced from her gums and two tiny fangs slid into place. Rolling onto her back, her head snapped and hit the stone floor with a crunch. Opening her eyes again, she felt her vision become blurred. The tiny veins in her eyes popped and exploded, sending blood gushing into the chocolate brown irises, but it quickly receded as the iris in each eye melted to a solid gold. As fast as they had changed to gold, they turned colors again. The color faded away, leaving her irises a pale blue that was almost gray. All at once, her body convulsed, then relaxed as she lost consciousness.

Standing up, One looked down at Saint with satisfaction. Looking to his right, it saw each of the council members standing over their students in much the same way. Three had a bit of a worried look spread across its face. "What happened?" One asked.

"The eyes did not revert to normal," Three said, shaking its head. "At least not yet."

One muttered a curse under its breath. Lifting its hand, it snapped its fingers once and pointed to the third student in line. The two attending Wraiths materialized out of the darkness and hovered around the student. Lifting slender, wooden stakes out of their gray and white coats, they stood silently above the unconscious boy. He was a young male of approximately twenty-five years with wavy brown hair. His white ceremonial robe was splattered angrily with his own blood as he lay motionless.

Three dropped down to its knees and rested a hand on the boy's head. "He's growing cold. We've lost him."

One shook its head. "Not everyone can handle the ritual. We always expect to lose one or two."

"I know," Three breathed, "but it never gets any easier." Lifting the boy's eyelid with its thumb, Three saw the solid gold eyes within. Standing up, Three took several steps away from the student. "Finish him before he wakes up. He wouldn't want to live like this."

The two Wraiths nodded. Dropping down to their knees, one reached in with his powerful hands and pinned the boy flat on his back, while the other pressed his knee firmly into the boy's chest. Lifting the stake over his head, the Wraith watched as the boy's eyes shot open. The glowing eyes snapped to the Wraith in instant anger. Struggling against the more powerful men, the newly created vampire shrieked in protest.

"Do it now!" Three commanded. "Do not let this abomination live!"

The Wraith brought the stake down swiftly, piercing the vampire's heart. The creature screamed in horror as blue flame leapt from the newly created wound and quickly began to engulf his entire body. Leaping away, the two Wraiths watched as smoke and cinders were thrown into the air as the vampire writhed on the floor. It was only moments before his body was reduced to ashes within the circle of candles.

"May God have mercy on our souls," One muttered. Looking up, he readdressed the council. "The ritual is complete. Let us retire and rest before the final test tonight." One turned his attention back to the two Wraiths. "Please attend to the students. Watch over them to make sure no one else turns."

The Wraiths nodded and set about their task. Moving to the right, one Wraith lifted Saint first and slung her over his shoulder like a doll. He could feel her warmth even through his clothing and smiled. Her body was in a state of flux, in the process of metamorphosis, and she would make a fine addition to the Gwyliad Wriaeth.

CHAPTER TWO

He pushed his body hard as he charged through the arched halls. Holding the gold embossed cylinder tightly in his left hand like a relay runner, he pumped his arms furiously. To a human's eye, he would be little more than a blur as he passed by, but his fellow vampires saw him coming and easily moved out of the way. As he turned the final corner, his shadow danced in and out of the moonlight spilling from the open windows as he headed toward the large, gilded doors at the end of the hall. The contents of the cylinder were far too important for electronic transmission. It could only be relayed by hand.

Slowing, he spotted two of the master vampire's more trusted men standing guard outside the door. These men had declared their loyalty to their master centuries ago and had never wavered in their resolve. Both were dressed in the same uniform—a long black coat that buttoned up the chest to the collar, yet hung loose past the waist down to their ankles—and were impressively imposing. With shaven heads, each wore a dark pair of wraparound sunglasses. The man on the left, a Caucasian standing close to six feet, had a long, red goatee that brushed against the collar of his coat. Dark tribal tattoos stretched from his temple down the left side of his face and disappeared below the collar of his coat. The other guard, a six and a half foot tall Asian man, had no facial hair but was covered with piercings. He had a row of sterling silver spikes implanted Mohawk style from the top of his forehead back to the base of his skull. A large silver ring hung from his nose and was connected by a chain to another in his bottom lip and three in his left ear. Both men looked as if they could kill with a single blow, although the courier knew it was only what they wanted him to see.

Stopping short, the courier lifted the embossed cylinder and showed it to the guards. "I have a delivery."

Steel Face nodded. "Our master is expecting you. He has been made to wait for some time."

"It wasn't easy getting here," the courier replied. "It is imperative that I be granted an audience with your master."

The two guards looked to each other, then stepped out of the way. Reaching back, they each pushed open a door with one of their meaty paws, revealing the chambers within. Golden flickering candlelight filtered over the immaculately decorated room. Rugs tastefully littered the floor among gothic furniture. Deep red and black, set against the white of the marble floors and walls, were the two overriding colors of the master's chamber. Several vampires stood around speaking in hushed tones, while numerous beautiful, scantily-clad women attended the Vampire Lord seated in a black throne at the rear of the room.

His throne was tall and thin, matching the vampire's own gaunt features. Its dark maroon and black veneer was intricately carved with images of death and lust. Two fanged skulls at the top of the throne stared down through ruby eyes at anyone who dared to stand before it. The Lord looked more like a grotesque statue than a living being. Not blinking, not breathing, the creature did not move. Swathed from head to foot in black silk, he was the very essence of regality and dignity. At his age, it was easier to wear actual clothes than to mentally project them. He did not even bother projecting a human form to those who looked upon him. He wore his vampirism like a badge of honor. A silver crown sat lightly upon his forehead and vanished into his wispy, graying hair that hung straight and long down over his shoulders. Several small, tight braids, created using tan twine, were hanging from his temples on both sides. His long, thin features and yellow eyes made him look more like a wicked farce of a human rather than one.

Rushing into the room, the courier's footsteps echoed loudly off the marble walls and floor. Quickly adjusting his leather coat and pushing his chin-length hair out of his face, he stopped just short of the throne and dropped to one knee. No guards approached him. He knew the master vampire had no true need for them, but they were a formality of his position. The master vampire could shred the courier before he had a chance to attack. Lifting up the cylinder, the courier presented it in his outstretched hand. "Lord Krath, I bear a message from Lord Stephanov." He held the posture without wavering. To do anything else would be an insult. A bead of sweat rolled down his forehead.

Krath moved his hand up from the armrest to his face, assuming a thoughtful position. Slowly, his yellow gaze fell down upon the courier and seemed to burn straight through the younger vampire. "So," his deep voice resonated off the walls of the room, "Stephanov sends word. And what would my enemy have to say to me?" His every move coldly calculated, he lifted his free hand and extended it palm up toward the courier.

Bowing his head, the courier placed the cylinder in Krath's hand.

Studying the cylinder for a moment, Krath traced over several of the intricate designs with his clawed fingers. It was stunningly beautiful, yet the ancient vampire knew beauty was most often the mask of treachery. His clan had been at war with Stephanov's for more decades than even he could remember now and the raison d'être seemed a dark, murky memory at this point. Lifting the cylinder to his nose, he took a deep whiff. He could detect no powder or resin that would signal the presence of explosives. Satisfied that it was nothing more than the courier indicated, Krath broke the seal. Sliding his fingers inside, he pulled free a heavy piece of parchment and unrolled it. Glancing over the meticulously crafted letter, Krath looked up with a mixture of pleasure and confusion on his face. Springing from his throne with a speed and excitement that seemed unbefitting his stature, the ancient vampire pointed to three of his servants on the far side of the room. "Gather everyone. I have news. Quickly now!"

The three vampires took no time in heading out of the throne room.

Krath looked over the letter again, then realized he was standing in front of the courier. "You, what is your name?"

"Sang," the courier replied without looking up or changing his position. Another bead of sweat formed on his forehead, just beside the intricate tribal tattoos that ran down his face.

"Sang?" Krath spat the name as if it were a bad taste in his mouth. A spark or recognition passed over his face for a moment. "Have I not heard your name before?" he asked mostly to himself. He paused and reflected before continuing. "You serve Stephanov?"

"No, my Lord," Sang responded. "I am merely a courier. I hold no allegiances."

Krath stared down at the young man before him. Protocol called for him to kill the vampire, but there was something about this vampire...he couldn't put his finger on it. Plus, Krath knew he needed to respond to the letter. "Stand up," he commanded.

Sang complied fearfully, but accepted his fate.

"I need you to take a message back to Stephanov," Krath stated.

Sang's eyes widened for a moment, but he quickly washed the surprise from his face. "Yes?"

Krath held the letter tightly in his hand. Looking down at the young vampire before him, he reached out and patted him gently on the shoulder. "Tell Stephanov that I accept."

Sang nodded.

"Be off," Krath instructed. "Make haste, Sang."

The courier wasted no time in turning and running out of the throne room. As he exited, he passed a multitude of vampires heading in.

Krath stood in front of his throne and addressed his assembled clan. Holding the letter aloft, he smiled, bearing his fangs. "Stephanov sends word."

A murmur ran over the crowd. This was unheard of.

"Some say our two clans have been warring since man first learned to walk upright, yet no longer can we afford this bloodshed. Our once proud covens have been utterly decimated by this feud. Stephanov has seen the error of his ways. He has offered to meet so we can negotiate peace. Europe will be ours again!" Krath's voice boomed.

The clan erupted into a wild chorus of cheers and applause.

"We must begin preparations for this meeting immediately," Krath continued. "My friends, my family, we are witnessing a historic event. Let no one convince you otherwise."

***

She awoke in a cold sweat. Sitting up straight, she pushed off the blanket carefully laid over her. Still dressed in her blood-splattered white ceremonial robe, Saint swung her legs over the edge of her bed and placed her head in her hands. Trying to push away the fog that had settled on her brain, she rubbed her eyes with the heels of her palms. She took a deep breath as she glanced around her room. Dusk had settled, casting yellow and orange rays in through her windows. Through the rays of light, she could see the dust motes wafting slowly through the air.

Standing up, she felt a twinge of pain in her neck. As she steadied herself against the frame of her bed, she placed her hand on her throat. She could feel the remains of the cut from the ceremony earlier in the day. The wound had already healed considerably and would be nearly gone by the next sunrise. She suddenly became aware that she wasn't quite herself anymore—not different, yet not the same. Lifting off her robe, she exposed her nude body to the golden light. Walking slowly across the floor, she stared at herself in the mirror attached to the back of her door. It was one of the few luxuries the council had granted her in her time at the academy.

She glanced over her toned, athletic twenty-three year old body. It didn't look any different to her, not externally anyway, yet it was. She stared for a moment at the blood caked on her forehead and in her hair. Rubbing her fingertips over it, she flaked off a bit, but she needed a shower to remove the rest. Leaning forward, she placed her palms flat on the mirror and rested her forehead on the cool glass. She noticed for the first time how her irises had changed. Formerly colored a deep brown, they were now a faded blue, bordering on gray.

"I look spooky," she laughed uncomfortably.

It was then she noticed her other cosmetic difference. Straightening up in front of the mirror, she lifted her upper lip to reveal two small fangs in place of her upper canines. Cocking her head to the right, she ran her thumb over the tip of one of her fangs, but quickly pulled it away with a yelp. Looking down, she saw a bead of blood welling up.

Licking it off quickly, she returned her attention to the new fangs. They extended almost a quarter of an inch past her incisors, but fit neatly over her bottom teeth when she bit down. Looking at them from all angles, she finally closed her mouth. They made her feel uncomfortable. Now, more than ever, she resembled the prey she was sworn to hunt and destroy. Stepping to her right, she moved fully into the remaining sunlight filtering in through her window—if only to make sure she didn't burst into flames. As the warmth caressed her body, she found some relief. Still human, she thought. Well, nearly human, she corrected.

A knock on her door startled the young woman. Grabbing her discarded robe from the floor, she pulled it on while assuring her visitor that she was coming. Rushing toward her dorm room door, she caught a glimpse of the darkening bloodstain running down the front of her robe. It was much larger than she originally thought. Feeling quietly self-conscious, she shook her head and reached for the doorknob. Pulling it open slowly, she found herself smiling brightly.

Reaching out, she jumped giddily into the arms of her visitor. "I did it!"

Returning the embrace of his student, Master Wraith Ben Quinn patted the young girl on the back and sat her down. Neither hulking nor imposing in his stature, his face and movements instead showed the wisdom of his age. His slight Asian heritage could be detected around his eyes and mouth, but was subdued by the spiky dark brown hair atop his head and the thick goatee that splayed out from his mouth in two solid straight lines and cut back beneath his chin toward the back of his face. A long braid of hair with numerous colored bands was tucked behind his left ear and hung down to the collar of his coat. Saint had helped him tie many of the colored bands into his braid, each a sign of a trial completed, or a vampire killed. His dark black trench coat was battered and torn from years of service, yet he would not be seen without it. Placing his hand on Saint's shoulder in a very fatherly gesture, he smiled at his protégé. "I knew you could."

The two walked into Saint's room and sat down on opposing sides of the space, much as they had done a hundred times before. They had not seen each other for almost three weeks, and after spending five years in the field together, each could feel the hole in their lives. Saint adored and admired Quinn, and he felt the same for her. He had grown from her instructor to the father figure she had craved in her life. At least a hundred years her elder, his dedication to the Guard had ensured that his intentions were always true. He was an excellent teacher as well. Always explaining anything he did, rather than just doing for his student, he forced her to dig her hands in and solve problems for herself.

"It's been weird without you," Saint admitted as she sat cross-legged on the bed with her robe pulled down over her knees. "I keep expecting you to be there when I turn around."

"I know the feeling," Quinn acknowledged. "When you spend five years with someone day in and day out, you grow," he rubbed his goatee as he searched for the proper word, "accustomed to their presence." He folded his arms across his chest and sat back in the wooden chair he had chosen. "But for each beginning, there is an end," he reminded her. "And for each ending, there is a beginning."

Saint nodded. It was a lesson he had taught her before. She never seemed to understand the meaning behind it, but she was starting to.

"There has been one nice thing about you being gone, though."

Saint's mouth fell open. "What? What is it?"

Quinn smiled slyly. "I've had the bathroom all to myself. It's been nice."

"Jerk!" Saint snatched her pillow up and flung it across at her mentor.

Easily grabbing it out of the air, Quinn set it on the floor next to him. He didn't want to return her ammo, just in case.

"So what have you been up to lately?" Saint asked.

"The council has been pressuring me to take another apprentice," he dismissed the concern with a wave of his hand. "I'm just not ready to repeat the whole process again. I mean, after you, I could use a vacation."

"Ha, ha," Saint said dryly.

Quinn nodded once to dismiss his comment as a joke. Saint easily understood. Over their time together, they had developed a sort of communication shorthand. Excess words were no longer needed, yet when they wanted to have a conversation, they could. Of the three students

Quinn had trained in his career, he had never grown as close to any of them as he had to Saint. He couldn't exactly put his finger on it, but they worked fluidly together, accentuating each other's positives and canceling out the negatives. He secretly hoped she would choose to continue working with him, rather than going solo as most young Wraiths did. He wasn't sure if he should press the point, or just let her make her own decisions though.

"How are you feeling?"

Saint forced a smile. "A little ookie, but okay. I'm not sure how I feel about the fangs, though."

Quinn cocked his head slightly to the right and sat forward. "You have fangs?"

Her Master's question surprised her. "Don't you?"

Quinn shook his head. "No. Fangs are something that only develops much later in a Wraith's life. Let me see."

Saint sat forward and lifted her upper lip.

Placing his hands on her face, Quinn examined the newly sprouted fangs. "That's the damndest thing, isn't it?" The expression on his face instantly melted from curiosity to concern as he sat back in his seat. "The council cleared you after the ritual?"

"I would assume," Saint said, "or else I would be a pile of ash on the floor, wouldn't I?"

Quinn laughed uncomfortably. "I imagine so."

The two sat in silence for a long moment.

"What?" Saint finally asked.

"You shouldn't have fangs," Quinn answered quickly.

"What are you trying to say?"

Quinn turned away from his student. Hitting his fist on his knee, he finally worked up the courage to say what was on his mind. "Something went wrong with your ritual."

His statement hit Saint like a semi-truck. "I don't understand."

Quinn reached over and took his apprentice tenderly by the hand. "No Wraith is born with fangs," he stated slowly. "The virus that created us was originally vampiric."

The statement was shocking, but not completely unexpected. It was simply a matter of looking at the oldest of the Wraiths to see that they were somehow related to vampires. Saint nodded for Quinn to continue.

"It isn't known for sure, but we think that one of the original members of our order must've contracted the vampirism virus while fighting them. Instead of changing this Wraith into a vampire, something strange happened. He gained all of the vampire's strengths and none of their weaknesses."

"How did it happen?" Saint asked. The ancient lore of the Gwyliad Wriaeth was a carefully guarded secret. It was not taught in any lecture hall, or written in any text that could be studied. To hear this from her Master's mouth was something of a revelation.

"It isn't truly known," Quinn answered, not fully aware of the whole tale himself. What he did know, he had haphazardly pieced together over his long lifetime. "The vampire and Wraith viruses are nearly identical, yet they do contain key genetic differences." Quinn sat back, carefully observing his student. "Does any of this sound familiar?"

Saint shook her head, enraptured by the tale.

"Are you sure?"

"No, why?"

Quinn bit his lip, then sat forward again. "Vampires are born with genetic memory," he said quickly. "Wraiths are not. That is one of the differences in the two viruses."

"What do you mean?"

"When a vampire is created, they know everything every one of them in their bloodline knew at the moment the virus was transmitted," Quinn said slowly. "That's why there's no need for any written records of their history. As soon as a new leech is created, they instantly know everything that every vampire before them knew."

"Wow," Saint breathed. "That would be handy. No need for training anymore. Just add blood and bang," she clapped her hands together, "instant Wraith."

Quinn chuckled. "Right, but it also tends to have its downsides. That much information that quickly usually serves to drive the new vampire completely insane." He was feeling a bit more at ease with his student again. He knew she was herself. "This is why very few vampires have the stamina for immortality."

"So the vampire virus is actually the older of the two viruses," Saint asked.

"Technically," Quinn thought for a moment, "but that's not the whole story. You see," he leaned forward and lowered his voice, "the Wraith are to blame."

"For what?"

"Vampires."

Saint sat back and looked oddly at her mentor. "Um, yeah. What?" She shook her hands. "How could we be to blame for vampirism, if it's actually the older of the viruses?"

"You see—"

A knock on the door startled both. They knew they were discussing a taboo subject and quickly became silent. Saint looked apologetically at her Master as she hopped up from the bed. Rushing across the room, she grabbed the door handle and pulled open the door impatiently. "Wha—?" She stopped herself short.

Standing outside her door was one of the council's inner circle of Wraiths. Dressed immaculately, he wore a maroon tunic below his gray coat, an indicator of his position. "Acolyte St. Louise, your final test begins in ten minutes. You are to meet me outside the compound, or you forfeit the test." The High Wraith looked passed Saint. His eyes focused on Quinn. "Master Quinn, your presence is also requested for this test. Please follow me."

Quinn stood up and nodded. Lifting his hand, he patted Saint's back. "Good luck." He smiled. Turning away, he left Saint alone in her room to prepare for her upcoming test.

***

Stephanov threw open the doors of his personal

chambers and marched angrily into the main room of the mansion, his black coat flowing majestically behind him. In his hand, he held an embossed gold cylinder, a scroll of paper folded hastily inside. "I will not even consider this!" Looking down at the cylinder, rage gripped him. Rearing back, he flung it hard into the wall.

By every account, Stephanov looked like the stereotypical "Hollywood Vampire." He continuously projected the image of perfectly white porcelain skin over his tall, lithe frame. His deep, rich eyes were colored an unnatural red, matching the maroon tie he wore knotted at his throat. Adjusting the collar of his exquisitely tailored black Italian suit, he pulled his knee-length jacket tighter around his strapping chest. His hair fell nearly to the center of his back, yet he pulled it tightly into a ponytail, only allowing several strands on both sides to frame his face. A pair of black leather gloves hid his slender, clawed hands, while only the smallest tuft of facial hair clung to his lower lip.

One of his assistants marched hurriedly behind him, doing her best to attend to her lord. "The message was hand delivered," the young woman urged. She was extraordinarily beautiful with her wavy chocolate hair, ashen skin, and cocoa colored eyes. Wearing a simple green cotton dress, she was the epitome of the-girl-next-door image. "I beg you to reconsider."

"I will do no such thing," Stephanov growled.

Walking across the gothic main room of his mansion, Stephanov headed toward the French doors on the far side. His image, his home, everything about this vampire was ripped straight from the pages of Bram Stoker's Dracula. Tall candelabras stood in the corners, each with slender white candles burning in them casting flickering golden light across the darkened room. Spider webs clung to high corners of the room, while ancient paintings hung below them silently observing the occupants of the home. Stephanov made sure, even though it was available, no electricity powered his home.

Pushing open the glass doors, Stephanov stepped into the cool night air of his second floor balcony. Moving to the edge, he placed his gloved hands on the iron rails and looked out over his property. Rolling hills stretched off to the east while groves of olive trees grew in his courtyard below. He took a deep breath of the sweet Italian air and let it soothe his anger. This place had been his home since before it had a name, and that would never change. He was born here, and then reborn into darkness in this place. He had traveled the world in his life of darkness, but no place on Earth could soothe him as his home did.

"This is treachery," Stephanov assured. "And that you would even ask I consider it questions your loyalty, Brigitte."

Brigitte shook her head in dismay. "How can you question me, my Lord? I have served you loyally for centuries." Her voice was soft and calm. "I only ask that you meet with Krath and hear what he has to say."

"And what would I have to say to the man who killed my wife?" Stephanov asked. "Should I smile, nod, and shake hands with this being, when I would rather spit in his eye and tear out his heart with my own hands?" Stephanov turned angrily toward Brigitte. "Is this what you would ask of me?"

Brigitte's face grew determined. "Yes! Yes, this is what you should do!" Her fear of this man diminished beneath her hope for the future. "How can you not even consider the possibility of bringing peace to our clans? We would put an end to the bloodshed. Is that not worth it?"

Stephanov stared at her, his red eyes growing in intensity, yet he could not bring himself to discipline her. More times than not, she had been the voice of reason in his life. Biting his lip, he stepped close to his assistant and placed his hand gently on her face. "How can I do this?"

"It is not a matter of how," Brigitte pointed out, "it is a matter of why." She cupped his hand in hers and stared directly into his eyes. "You lost your beloved wife to this war with Krath. Each of us has lost someone special. Krath has obviously come to understand this. Hear him out, my Lord. That's all I ask."

He glanced lovingly at his assistant. He was her creator. He loved her the way a father would. He had raised her and taught her the way of the vampire. How could he not hear her pleas now? "Give me some time to consider the proposal."

Brigitte smiled. Rushing forward, she hugged him tightly. "Thank you, my Lord."

Stephanov returned the embrace. Turning his head, he stared up at the full moon hovering in the sky. As it cast its silvery light down over his land, he couldn't help but feel his heart sinking in his chest. He would never be able to avenge his wife's death now. He would be forced to smile at the man who had personally executed her. If there was to be peace among the vampire nation, it would be his generation that would have the hardest time living in it.

CHAPTER THREE

Saint had heard stories from the other Wraith Acolytes, but now it was her turn to learn firsthand, or die trying. This was her trial by fire, as it were. If she passed, she would be awarded her status as a full Wraith and her life. If she were to fail this test…well, it was best not to think about that. There was already enough pressure on her without worrying about dying in a school exam.

Pulling her dark gray trench coat tightly around her thin frame, she walked briskly into the biting wind, still weary from the events earlier in the day. Her long, wavy, raven hair whipped behind her as she buried her face in the collar of the coat. She thought briefly about how much she hated this color on her. She couldn't wait to graduate, then she could pick her own clothes. No more robes and cloaks. She could finally wear what she wanted. Her mind drifted back to the task at hand as her blue-gray eyes focused on her destination.

Her newly enhanced senses keenly aware, she felt the surveillance. They had been ghosting her for some time, weaving in and around buildings, trying not to give themselves away. She let a smile creep across her full lips. She had noticed them as soon as they had begun tracking her. Two were instructors at the academy, but the other was a bit more…elusive. It was her mentor, Master Wraith Ben Quinn. He had evaded her detection for quite a while, but had given up his position about a half a mile back when he knocked a brick loose from a high ledge. She wondered if he had done this intentionally, as if he were simply reassuring her that he was there without breaking the rules of the test. Without another thought, she knew this to be true.

The sound of her boot heels clicking against the cobblestone streets boomed loud in her ears as she neared the test area. She could feel her heart thumping in her chest, threatening at any moment to burst free and scurry away. But she was a Wraith—or at least almost. Fear was her adversary, first and foremost. If she succumbed to it, she was dead. There was no margin of error in the task ahead. No second chances. Pulling her slender hands free of the charcoal gray coat, she wrapped them gently around two iron bars of the large fence that surrounded the entire complex. It was nearly eight feet tall in most areas, but some of the fence had begun to sink and collapse due to the ground it was built upon. Glancing into the eastern sky, she watched as the last shades of yellow, orange and red faded beyond the rolling ocean. The test began promptly at sundown.

Dropping down gracefully to her knees, she straightened her back and rested her hands on her thighs. Twisting her neck around slowly, she could feel the tension in it. She had been training almost non-stop for the past three weeks for this test alone. There was no curriculum to study, no controlled environment, and no instructors standing nearby to keep her safe. This was everything she had been trained to do the past ten years, all at once. Closing her eyes for a moment, she took a breath in through her nose and exhaled deeply to center herself.

It was time.

Saint stood and addressed her target. Reaching out her hand, she grasped the gate and drug it open. It creaked and moaned as the rusty hinges moved for the first time in years. Stepping inside, she felt a cold shiver run down her spine. It was in there. She could sense it. Moving her hand inside her coat, she pulled a small, cylindrical object free of her belt. As she held it tightly, she could feel its power pulsing off the warm metal. When it was in her hands, she felt complete—she felt powerful. It was no longer just her weapon, but an extension of herself. She would feel no more comfortable without it, than if she had lost a limb. This was the only tool she needed to complete her test. It had served her well these past ten years and would not fail her now. But as with any tool, she reminded herself, it's only as useful as the person who wields it. This was a test for her, not her weaponry.

Glancing up, Saint looked upon her target as if for the first time. She had spent many cool summer nights playing here as a child, but that was before the darkness came. The other children spun stories of a horrible ogre who lived there now, and who would eat any kids who were foolish enough to step foot inside the gates. Well, she thought, at least they had part of the story right. The tall, cylindrical building stretched high into the sky, a reminder of Queen Anne's once proud English kingdom nearly three hundred years ago. This lone battlement had stood watch over the rolling waves of the coast against any invading forces. Saint was unsure if this place ever saw any battles, nevertheless, time had not been kind to it. How it still stood was a mystery to many, and a constant concern to the townsfolk. The brick and mortar walls of the building had begun to crumble and the battlements above had long since caved in, or fallen to the ground. The constant erosion of the cliff on which it was built was another concern. It was more likely to fall into the ocean than cave in at this point.

Her eyes wandered down the side of the building toward the base. The door, nothing more than an arch, was boarded up to prevent any unauthorized access. She had been there on the day the boards had been riveted into place. Standing against the gate with her mum's hand caressing the back of her head, she watched as her castle was taken away. With tears in her eyes, she saw the men of the town swathed in crucifixes and garlic working feverishly as they glanced nervously into the tower. That day would be forever etched in her mind as the last board was slammed into place. A beloved part of her childhood had been unfairly taken away and she never knew why. As she stood outside the ancient watchtower now, she understood. It was why this place was chosen for her.

Curling her fingers around the first plank, Saint tore it away from the wall with her preternatural strength. Piece by piece, she tore the barricade down until the entrance was cleared. As she stepped inside, she expected bats to come screaming out of the darkness at any moment as their sanctum was violated. But there was nothing. Peering up through the darkness, she could vividly remember the details of the battlement. A set of stairs crawled up the inner wall toward the second story barracks and then onto the watchtower above. Broken stones and support beams littered the floor of the building, as did semi-crushed beer cans and discarded pieces of clothing.

Moving carefully to the steps, Saint began to make her way toward the barracks. Its presence was there. She had felt it growing stronger, even as she entered the grounds. It knew she was here, too, but had made no attempt at evasion. It was waiting for her. A rush of adrenaline hit her as she neared the entrance to the barracks. Her hand ran against the curved outer wall, her fingernails clicking against the stones. Grabbing her long, gray coat, she threw it off her shoulders exposing the black tank top and jeans she wore beneath. Her brain swam with a mixture of excitement and fear, intoxicating her senses. Lifting her silver weapon up, she thumbed the single activation button on the hilt. The weapon spring to life, instantly quadrupling in length. Two silver stakes sprouted from both ends as it gleamed in the low light. Cradling the weapon in her hands, she tapped the activation button again. A long, thin, curved blade snapped up from the head of the staff with a satisfying clang. Holding her scythe aloft, she quickly took the three final steps up to the barracks.

The overpowering stench of death hit her nostrils hard, almost forcing her to vomit. Clenching her teeth, she pushed the distraction away and stepped inside. On the far side of the room, she could see a second set of stairs that led to the tower, while three cots were scattered messily about the room. A large, gaping scar was carved into the wooden floor allowing her to stare back into the murky depths of the battlement. Debris from the crumbling roof above littered the floor, as did several decaying body parts. Focusing all of her senses, she scanned the room. It was here, but where? Taking a step further into the room, she stopped and closed her eyes. She would make it come to her.

Whipping her scythe around her body with a flourish, Saint slammed the tip into the rotting floorboards. With her weapon standing erect, she sank to her knees to meditate again. Closing her eyes, she immediately began an exercise she was taught at the academy. Saint channeled her energy inward amplifying her senses. Reaching out, she explored every darkened corner of the room. Sweeping the crumbling room with her senses, she hit a cold spot and smiled. Stopping the sweep, she slowly opened her eyes and looked directly toward the spot she had uncovered.

She slowly slipped her hand into her rear pant pocket. "Come out and play," she cooed.

Her eyes still firmly focused on the spot, she pulled her hand free and stood up. She spotted a shimmer in the darkness. It was camouflaged, but moving toward her. It had the ability to not only take on human form, but also, like a chameleon, mimic its environment. This explained all those myths and legends of the creatures just disappearing in a wide-open space. It was also one hell of an offensive technique. But she was on to it.

Much like a bloodhound with a scent, Saint was locked on. Her ears strained against the hollow darkness, catching every scrape of a fingernail, or the rustle of cloth. She could even detect the faint swoosh of blood through the ventricles of the creature's heart. Lifting up her hand, she sharpened her eyes.

"Tag!" she yelled while flinging two four-inch steel projectiles at the creature.

A shriek sliced like a razorblade through the silence as the two spikes hit the creature squarely in the back. Losing its mental focus, its camouflage melted away revealing the horrible, gray corpse beneath. As it dropped to the floor in front of Saint, she could see that the years of decay had rotted away its lips and portions of its cheeks, leaving its fanged mouth in a permanent grotesque sneer. As it jostled for position in front of her, she realized that it was languid and tired. It had not fed in some time. Its gold eyes seemed dull as it stared. It was dying. It had nothing to lose.

Saint held her ground. She knew the creature would fight relentlessly to defend its meager life and nest. Her mouth became dry as she looked over the monster before her. She had never encountered a vampire in an uncontrolled environment such as this. Each time before, she had her Master by her side. She was alone now and suddenly, the five foot nine being before her towered over her. She glanced to her scythe, not more than an arm's length away, but it seemed more like a mile.

"Where's your sharp tongue now, Wraith?" the vampire hissed in an odd accent, probably due to its lack of lips. "Have you no witty comeback now?"

Saint grinned. "I just couldn't get past how ugly you are."

The vampire hissed and charged. Instantly leaping into the air, Saint had retrieved her scythe and bounded over the creature. With speed and strength every bit as enhanced as her prey, the two were an even match. Reversing his attack, the vampire brought its razor-sharp claws down across Saint's chest, cleaving open three wounds just above her breasts. The young Wraith Acolyte grunted as blood spilled down her torso. Pushing past the pain, she focused on the vampire.

Lifting its hand, the monster licked the blood from its claws, all while glaring at Saint. "They say a Wraith's blood created us." It moaned in pleasure. It smiled—well, at least as well as it could. "I just think it tastes great."

Saint sneered. Swinging the silver blade across and down, she connected with the vampire instantly severing the limb just above the elbow. She watched in awe for a moment as the arm burned almost instantly to ash as it hit the floor. With the creature stumbling, Saint pressed her attack. Digging the scythe's point into the floor, she vaulted forward and hit the vampire in the chest with her feet. As the creature recoiled, Saint pulled her weapon free and brought it down over her head. The creature's golden eyes widened in horror as the blade sliced cleanly through its chest.

The vampire tried to recover but it was too late. Blue flame began to burn across the wound as smoke and glowing red embers were spit into the air. Bringing her scythe around, Saint twirled it twice in front of her chest as she watched the vampire begin to burn. Twisting her head around, she felt her neck pop twice. Sighing, she snapped the scythe up and jabbed it straight into the creature's chest, piercing its heart. The vampire wailed in pain and agony as his body convulsed. An eerie blue light began to shine from inside its mouth as its body tore itself apart. Falling back to the floor, the nearly skeletal form shattered and crumbled upon impact, sending a plume of flame and ash into the air.

As the smoke began to clear, Saint strode confidently over the body of her kill toward the exit. "And stay down." She laughed devilishly.

Tapping the activation button on her scythe's grip, the weapon snapped shut and reverted to its original, compact form. She stowed it neatly on her belt as she made her way down the stairs. Reaching the bottom, she retrieved her standard issue gray coat and pulled it on. As she stepped into the chilled English air, a smile grew wide across her slender face. She had done it. She had passed the final test. Taking a deep breath, she felt the wind whip across her sweaty skin. She couldn't help but giggle in sheer joy.

It was the culmination of ten years of training. Emily St. Louise was a Wraith now.

***

Night had just fallen when the first vampire arrived. Pulling up in black luxury sedans, they

51

were careful to align their headlights into the open field that had been selected for the meeting. Trees and brush lined all sides of the plain, except for two small dirt access roads leading in. One by one, the vampires exited their vehicles and began to gather behind the row of parked cars. As the final car in their convoy came to a stop, the first twinkle of headlights could be seen on the opposite side of the field. Heavy storm clouds had rolled in just before dusk, obscuring the stars and moon, making it pitch black outside. Only the random brief blue-white flash of lightning illuminated the vampires. A few sparse drops of rain had been falling, but the clouds had yet to unleash the storm it had been threatening the area with.

As an attendant opened his car door, Krath stepped out into the night, the wind tossing his wispy hair in all directions. Using his decaying hand to lay it flat to his scalp, he looked up into the darkened skies, his golden eyes luminous in the low light. "Weather like this makes you feel alive," he said to everyone and no one in specific. His black silk robes billowed in the wind, making him look more like an apparition than a physical being as he moved to the front of the vehicles. His legs sliced through the headlights as another bolt of lightning rolled across the sky. Stopping in the center, he squinted his eyes slightly to see multiple figures moving in the dark across the way. It was Stephanov's men.

As the headlights crisscrossed the field, two distinct groups could be seen on each side. Stephanov's men reflected his style, each meticulously groomed, dressed in formal suits and long coats. Krath's men, on the other hand, had adopted more of a modern gothic style, heavy on black leather and silver jewelry. Both sides were represented by ten to fifteen of the Vampire Lord's closest, and most trusted, men. Even though the message to both sides had requested they show up unarmed, every vampire standing on that field was concealing an arsenal of weapons. They would not walk blindly into any situation and leave their lord unprotected. Each side stood for what seemed like an eternity. Neither was willing to make the first move.

Pulling off his dark sunglasses, Stephanov decided to move first. With two guards flanking him on either side, he strode confidently toward the center of the field. If it were truly to be a new era of peace, chances would have to be taken. He would not let any vampire say that he was unwilling to bring an end to the war. He was proud and sometimes headstrong, but he was no fool. Neither side could afford the hostilities any longer, no matter what personal aspirations each leader harbored. Stopping in the middle, he waited.

Krath's face was unemotional at the display, but those closest to him knew he was pleased. By far the elder of the two lords, Krath had already conquered, relinquished, and reconquered entire empires before Stephanov was even born. A native of Eastern Europe, he knew the truth about the original vampires of Transylvania, but would take that knowledge to his grave. With a nod, he instructed his personal guards to lead the way. As they moved ahead, three more guards took up position behind their lord. Looking more like members of the Secret Service than vampires, they each wore dark glasses and earpieces to monitor the transmissions of other guards.

As the two Vampire Lords approached each other, a spring of hatred welled up in Stephanov. He knew the man before him was a monster, and made no attempts to cover it. Gritting his teeth, he swallowed the anger down and bottled it. He swore that peace or no peace, someday, he would have vengeance. Stephanov extended his hand to his enemy. "Good to see you again, Krath."

Krath accepted the hand and shook it firmly. "Likewise," he purred in his Eastern European accent.

Both had chosen to speak English during the talks, though it was not the native, or secondary language of either. Both found the language spoken in England's colonies to be too simplistic and unemotional for their personal taste, but it had been chosen as the tongue of diplomacy because of that fact.

"Where do we begin?" Krath asked, his gold, unblinking eyes focused on his adversary.

Stephanov licked his dry lips. "I don't know." It had been almost two days since he had fed. He was weary and stressed. He was not making good decisions. "An apology?"

Krath's face remained unchanged. "From me? For what?"

"You know damn well for what," Stephanov spat. He couldn't hide the venom that had built up over the centuries for the vampire standing before him. "You killed my wife!" Brigitte, standing behind her master, reached out and placed a hand on Stephanov's shoulder to calm him. Angrily brushing her hand away, he stared intently at his enemy.

Krath rolled his eyes to the right and tilted his head back slightly. "Ah," he recalled, "that's what started this war."

"Don't play dumb with me, Krath."

"My Lord, no," Brigitte said softly. "We are here for peace."

Stephanov shot an angry glance over his shoulder, silencing his attendant.

"I had forgotten," the elder vampire stated slowly. "It has been so long ago." Krath's golden eyes seemed to dim for a moment. "There are a great many things I regret," he said to the awe of both sides, "and that is one of them." He slowly reached out and placed his hand on Stephanov's shoulder. "Please forgive me, my friend."

Stephanov moved away from Krath's touch. "I cannot. I will not forgive you, Krath. Not ever."

Krath hung his head as the two clans stood silently. Slowly returning his gaze to Stephanov, a curious look washed over his face. "I do not understand," he said after a moment. "If you cannot see past your rage and anger, why did you initiate peace talks? Surely you would have known they would fail?"

Stephanov admitted to his own confusion. "I did not initiate this meeting," he said warily. "It was a message from you."

Krath shook his head. "I sent no such message."

The two vampire clans went on alert. Drawing their weapons, each clan backed away from the other. Another bolt of lightning tore across the sky as the rain began to pour down around them. It was then that a high-pitched whine sliced through the air. The two clans began to retreat to their vehicles sensing the danger, but it was too late. An explosive device ripped open the ground almost exactly where the two lords had been standing. The concussion blast threw bodies in all directions. Moments after the first bomb, other devices began to detonate in sequence, utterly obliterating all life on the field. A bomb exploded just inches from Stephanov, shredding his body. As the Vampire Lord fell dead to the ground, Krath laughed under his breath. Turning away from the scene, his guards hurriedly rushed him toward his car, but it was too late. A third sequence of bombs detonated, engulfing Krath's clan in a hellish fireball. As Krath burned, his fists clenched in anger. He was ash before he hit the ground. Smoke and fire rained down on the crater created by the blast among the charred corpses and destroyed vehicles. As the vampires burned, unearthly blue flame hastened their demise.

Amidst the wreckage and carnage, a lone survivor crawled through the smoke. Reaching her hand out, Brigitte tried to pull herself up. Her face was twisted with cuts and lacerations from the flying shrapnel and debris. Below the knee, her left leg had been completely excised by one of the explosions. Struggling to maintain her mental projection, she rolled onto her back in agony. Looking up through the smoke-filled sky, she saw a dark form moving toward her. Squinting her eyes, she saw it was a man swathed entirely in black with a long cape flowing behind him. Fear gripped her heart.

"Who…?" Brigitte croaked painfully.

"Your new lord," the man announced confidently. His voice was deep with jagged edges. The cape he wore stretched down from his neck and licked the ground at his feet. A hood was pulled up over his head leaving only his most striking feature exposed: a rusted, flat, silver faceplate that seemed to be riveted to his face. Two rectangular slits were cut, allowing his golden eyes to shine through signaling, at least, that he was a vampire. Three additional vertical cuts were aligned over the mouth of the mask. The figure stood nearly seven feet tall and appeared to be built like a Greek God. As he looked down at Brigitte, his eyes burned with intensity. "You serve me now."

PART TWO

One Truth...

It will not be easy.

Those you love will be taken from you as you walk the path.

The path is placed before you, and is yours alone. To walk it demands courage, strength, and resolve. To falter now is to lose everything. There is no correct path, no right answer.

It will not be easy.

CHAPTER FOUR

Saint lifted her glass in the air. "To Toby. He's in a better place now."

Each of the remaining six Wraiths, a smattering of Masters, and a few students lifted their glasses to echo the toast.

Tilting the glass back, Saint took a long drink of the amber colored alcohol. Wiping a bit of foam from her lips, she returned the glass to the bar and leaned forward. Glancing around the nearly empty tavern, she signaled the bartender to hit her again. As the burly, bearded man refilled her glass, Saint retrieved a few bills from her pocket and slid them toward him. Grabbing the money, the bartender nodded and walked away. Turning back to her fellow Wraiths, Saint forced a smile. Less than an hour ago, each had learned that Toby Adams didn't survive the previous day's ritual. He had been staked by the attending wraiths. It happened sometimes, she tried to tell herself, but that didn't make it any easier. She had grown up with Toby. He was a young man from Southern England who looked to have a bright future. To know that he had been unceremoniously killed on the council floor when the Wraith virus didn't take was a shock to them all.

But this was a happy occasion. They were celebrating their graduation this night. Each had recovered from the ritual and passed the final test set before them by the council. They were Wraiths now, awaiting their first assignments. Much like soldiers completing basic training, they each knew they were about to be shipped off to different war zones, and would probably not see each other again. The statistics concerning a new Wraith surviving their first year of solo duty weren't impressive. They weren't good at all. It was best to celebrate their commencement before they were moved to the front line.

Lifting the fresh beer to her lips, Saint was very careful to hide her fangs. Her conversation a day earlier with her Master had made her very self-conscious about them. Currently working on her fourth beer, she was becoming slightly less concerned, though. "So what are everyone's plans?" she asked as she sat back on her padded barstool.

"To get so fucked up, that I have to be carried out of here!"

Everyone laughed at Sam's statement. Sam DeMoro—the obligatory class clown—was in rare form tonight. Dressed in his normal street clothes consisting of a black t-shirt and blue jeans, he was hanging off the end of the bar. A lightweight by any standard, he had been two-fisting beers and shots of straight whiskey all night. He was already well on his way to meeting his prediction.

"I just want to enjoy you guys while we're all still together," Gunter Reinhart stated soberly. The second youngest of the graduating class at twenty-four, he had been admitted to the Academy when only nine years old. His family had been killed in a terrorist attack on the German Embassy in England. A friend of the family was a Master Wraith and offered to admit him to the Academy instead of placing him in foster care. Each of the other students had quickly adopted Gunter and had helped him through his difficult time. A sensitive and caring young man, he had excelled in his studies much in the same way Saint had.

"I agree," Sam stammered. "I think a game of naked Twister is in order," he said, looking directly at Saint.

Saint tilted her head to the right and smiled. "If you think you're man enough, Sammy."

Sam cocked an eyebrow at the invitation. Laughing, he tried to stand up, but instead, slipped off the barstool and tumbled to the ground with a thump.

"Well, he's out." Saint laughed.

Glancing over her shoulder, she stared at the front door expectantly. She had invited Master Quinn, but he had yet to show up. She quietly worried over her drink. It wasn't like him not to show. Punctuality was the tenet he built his life around. Returning her attention to the group, she spotted her best friend at the Academy sitting quietly two seats down nursing a warm beer. Lifting her drink from the bar, Saint turned toward him. "What's up, Miller?"

Miller Barnes looked up at his friend with a half-hearted smile. "Not a whole helluva lot. You?"

"I'm selling weapons to small third world countries to support their revolution," Saint answered matter-of-factly. "Business is good."

Miller stared at her a moment before laughing out loud. "What the hell is wrong with you?"

Saint rubbed his back. "Nothing more than

usual."

Miller was more to Saint than just her best friend. They had arrived at the Academy at just about the same time and had instantly bonded. The only American in the graduating class, Miller was her source for Western culture. They had experienced almost everything together. Miller had been Saint's first kiss one cool August night when she was fourteen. They had also been each other's first lovers. At one point, they had both talked of leaving the Academy and running away together, but their overriding sense of duty and a stern lecture from Master Quinn had prevented that. Attachment between Wraiths is not forbidden, but at the same time, it is not encouraged. The two had decided that their friendship was more important one night in Saint's dorm room as they watched the snow fall silently outside. As they laid in each other's arms the rest of the night, their bond was permanently forged. Besides Master Quinn, Saint cared the most for Miller.

Miller was much taller than Saint and built like a brick house. His wide, strapping chest was finely chiseled from his years of training and hard work. His dirty blond hair was closely cropped on the sides and back, but messy and a bit longer on top. Two stray locks of hair hung down over his forehead. Still wearing the gray coat the Wraith had given him, he had altered the uniform slightly to include a white button-up shirt, dark slacks, and a heavy pair of combat boots. His face was strong and hard with a beautiful jaw line, high cheekbones, and emerald, green eyes. He looked more like a model or actor than a hardened warrior.

Peeling the label from his bottle, he swallowed down the last bit of alcohol and turned to his friend. "I just don't think I'm ready for all this to be over."

"I see an empty table over there, you want to talk about it?"

Miller smiled at Saint. "Sure."

As the two moved away from the bar, they both took seats at a small, intimate table near the back of the tavern. A lone candle burned in a square glass in the center of the table casting long shadows on the wall behind them. Setting her glass down, Saint peered out a nearby window into the cool October night. She could see the lights from the rest of the town shining brightly under a crisp, starlit sky.

Reaching over, she took Miller's hand into hers. "Everything has an end," she said slowly.

"I know," Miller acknowledged, "but that doesn't mean I have to like it. For the past ten years, this Academy and you guys are all I've known. How do I start over?"

"Who says you have to?" Saint asked. "Just because we're all graduating doesn't mean that we'll never see each other again. We don't have to stop being friends."

"I guess," Miller stalled. "I guess I'm just scared."

Saint smiled softly. "Why?"

Miller looked up into her eyes and momentarily lost himself. Lifting himself out of the shimmering pools that were her new gray eyes, he faced his fears. "I don't want to die, Saint."

"None of us do," she admitted. "Honestly, I've

spent my share of nights worrying about this same exact thing, but I've come to one conclusion."

"What's that?"

"Death is inevitable for all of us," Saint answered. "I know that sounds grim, but it really isn't. We have to be reminded—especially at our age—that we aren't immortal." She clasped his hand tightly. "And that we have to live each moment to the fullest, not knowing how much time we may have left."

"You're right," Miller breathed.

"Damn right I am," Saint said confidently. "We have to live our lives like each day is our last and not worry about it."

"How do you not worry about it?"

"Skill mostly," she joked.

Miller laughed. "No, seriously."

Saint took a breath and paused for reflection. "You just can't. I don't know any other way of explaining it. Humans are born with built-in timers. Once our time is up, that's it. We have to try and use our lives as wisely as possible." She rubbed her thumb over the back of his hand softly. "Is any of this helping?"

Miller smiled, but shook his head. "No, but thanks for trying. I just have to come to grips with this by myself. Thanks, Saint."

"Anytime, sweetheart," she smiled. Sitting back, she found herself not wanting to let go of his hand. It had been quite a while since the last time they were together and she wanted him. Biting down on her bottom lip, she stared into his green eyes. He was everything she needed right now, everything she desired. Closing her eyes for a moment, she sighed softly. Pulling away her hand, she stood up. She couldn't. Not right now. Although somehow, deep in the back of her mind, it seemed completely appropriate. She wanted to just reach over and pull him from his seat and kiss him passionately, to drag him from the bar back to her dorm room and tear off his clothes. She craved him. Taking a deep breath, she tried to work up the courage.

Opening her mouth, she quickly tried to form the question in her mind. "You want," she paused, "another beer?"

"Yeah," Miller said, fully engrossed in peeling the last remaining shreds of paper from the bottle in front of him. "That sounds great."

Turning back toward the bar, she cursed herself under her breath. Chicken. Tilting her head back, she downed the last of her glass. Setting it on the bar, she signaled for the bartender to bring two more draughts. Maybe a little more liquid courage, she thought. As the bartender returned, Saint slipped some more cash his way and picked up the tall, curvy glasses. Turning back to the table, her heart dropped. Miller was gone. Setting the beers back on the bar, Saint rushed toward the door. Throwing it open, she stepped out into the night. Glancing around, she spotted Miller leaning against the wall of a nearby building lighting a cigarette.

She slowly walked toward him. "What the hell are you doing?"

Miller took a drag of the cigarette and slowly exhaled it. "I picked this nasty habit up from my

Master." He laughed. "God, I hate these things." He looked down at the cigarette in his hands. "But it's not like I'm going to die of cancer or anything."

"Not that," Saint said quickly. "Why did you walk out on me?"

Miller lowered his head. "I'm sorry. I just needed some air. I needed a little time to think."

"You want me to leave you alone?" Saint asked, hoping his answer would be no. As the moonlight reflected off his face, she wanted him even more.

Taking another drag of the cigarette, he flicked it into the street. "You know what I have in mind?"

"God, I hope so," Saint cooed.

Reaching out, Miller took Saint by the hand. Smiling slyly, he turned and walked between the buildings with her in tow. The small town that was home to the Academy sat on the English coast facing France. From the school, it was only two minutes to the ocean. Walking out of the city, Miller started toward the waterline. Heading down a small incline, the two stumbled onto the sandy beach just as the tide washed in.

Turning back to Saint, Miller placed his hands gently on her face and kissed her. Wrapping her arms around him, Saint melted. Gently grabbing her bottom lip with his teeth, she moaned gently. Using his thumb to push her head back, he kissed quickly down her chin to her throat. Running her hands up his back, she forcefully started to pull off his coat. Tossing it aside, Saint let her coat drop away as well. As his tongue flicked over her earlobe, she ran her hands over his well-defined chest and down to his waist. Grabbing his pants, she snapped open the top button and undid his fly. Pulling her head forward, she kissed him firmly, running her tongue over his lips. Sliding her hand down his pants, she was pleased to find his penis already erect. Rubbing it with the heel of her hand, she felt him move down toward her neck again. She wanted to go down on him, to take his stiff member into her mouth, but the thought of her new fangs changed her mind.

Saint pushed him away. Taking a step back, she reached down and pulled up her shirt. Working it easily off her arms and head, she tossed it to the sand exposing her breasts to the brisk night air. Her nipples already erect, she quickly flipped off her boots and started to work on her pants. Pulling off his shirt, Miller rushed in and took Saint's now naked body into his arms. His hand moved to her chest and he gently ran his fingertips over the three cuts just above her breasts.

He looked into her eyes. "How?"

She smiled. "Vampire got a lucky shot in." She laughed. "Just one though."

Miller smiled and leaned in for another kiss. Moving his hands lower, he cupped Saint's breasts. He could feel her firm nipples against his palms. She moaned in satisfaction. Reaching down, she pushed down his pants and underwear until they were both nude. Grabbing his hands, she led him down to the water's edge and pulled him down to the sand.

Lying on her back, she spread her legs and waited for him. On his knees just inches above her,

Miller dragged his erection through her soft pubic hair toward her vagina. He could feel the warmth between her legs as he inserted the head. Arching her back, Saint moaned loudly as the two became one. Their pelvises together, she wrapped her legs around his lower back. Leaning over, Miller kissed her breasts gently. Running his tongue over her nipples, he slowly began to rhythmically pump his hips. The alternating sensation of the cool air and her warmth only added to his excitement.

Wrapping her arms around his neck, Saint rolled Miller over and climbed on top. Grinding her pelvis into his, she took every bit of him inside her. Sitting up straight, she looked down at Miller with wicked pleasure. Running her hands up her body, she gently caressed her nipples as she moved. His hands on her hips, she began to move faster, their bodies in perfect rhythm. Dropping her head back, she moaned again as she felt his penis throb inside her. They were both close to orgasm. Falling forward, she sped up again, almost ready to burst. As she reached her climax, Saint cried out in pure pleasure as cold waves crashed into them. Rolling her over, Miller pumped hard against her, his godlike body flexing in the moonlight. With one final pump, he pushed hard against her as he ejaculated.

As he fell forward in exhaustion, Saint wrapped her arms around him, satisfied to have his naked body pressed against hers. As Miller slowly pulled free, he rolled onto the wet sand next to her. Reaching over, he took her hand in his.

"You know I love you," Saint said softly.

Miller nodded. Reaching over, he ran his fingertips across her forehead and into her hair. "I know."

The two let their heads fall back into the sand and stared up into the sky. It was a perfectly clear night and a million stars were visible. The moon shone brightly in the sky as it made its slow nightly journey toward the horizon. This would probably be the last time Miller and Saint saw each other. As Saint stared at the blanket of stars above her, she felt a general sense of peace. She knew everything was connected in some way and they would meet again.

Rolling onto her side, she propped her head up with her arm. Reaching over, she began to run her fingernails through his chest hair. "So," she breathed, "wanna go again?"

***

Master Ben Quinn stood outside the council chambers waiting impatiently. He should have been at Saint's graduation party almost two hours ago, but the members of the council had summoned him. Unsure of what they wanted to speak to him about, Quinn began to pace outside the doors. Clasping his hands behind his back, he glanced out a nearby window. The moon was high in the sky. It was nearing midnight. Stopping in midpace, he turned his back to the doors, took a deep breath in through his nose and tried to focus. His nervousness wasn't befitting a Wraith of his stature. He was acting like a first year Acolyte again.

Craning his head to the left and then the right, he relaxed the muscles in his neck. He heard a small pop in the upper vertebrae and stopped as a smile flashed across his face. He remembered how Saint would always pop her neck before charging into battle. A little on the reckless side, she was, nevertheless, courageous beyond her years. Perhaps that could be attributed to her lack of experience, but Quinn hoped his student never lost her drive and excitement...or her life. Gritting his teeth, his smile faded away. He couldn't bear the thought of losing her.

He hadn't truly realized it until they had spent time apart: She was the sun in his sky. Perhaps that was being a bit overdramatic, but she meant the world to him. Over the five years they had spent together, trudging through darkened alleys and fighting an unseen war, an understandable bond had been forged. Yet theirs ran deeper. Maybe it was because she was a woman and some prehistoric instinct to protect her had been tapped, but that could only be a part of it. A mutual respect and admiration had developed between the two. He, an enhanced human, and she, not, she still kept up with him on every mission, every hunt. His preternatural abilities augmented his healing abilities, strength, speed, and senses, while she was nothing more than a "normal" human being—if that term even applied anymore. He had seen her take down vampires faster than a full Wraith with none of the enhancements. She was truly a remarkable person.

There were those within the Gwyliad Wriaeth who sought to change the way Acolyte Wraiths were trained. They felt that sending a regular human out with a full Wraith was not only reckless, but also irresponsible. The students should be allowed to partake in the ritual before their five years of training in the field, but Quinn disagreed and Saint had repeatedly shown him why. To effectively wield the power of the Wraith, a person needed more than discipline and a scythe; someone who had plumbed the depths of their soul and found their true strength within was required. It was less about training than discovering one's true self. To this end, the five years of fieldwork was invaluable. Once an Acolyte returned and was ready to be turned, they already knew what they were capable of. The gifts bestowed by the Wraith virus were essentially only added bonuses for an already well-rounded soldier.

His thoughts were interrupted as the heavy council doors swung open behind him. Spinning on his heels, he watched two maroon-vested High Wraiths appear from the darkness and motion him inside. Following them into the pitch-black chamber, Quinn walked steadily to keep pace. The High Wraiths knew every inch of this room by heart. They could probably walk the perimeter of the council chamber blindfolded and never hit anything. Of course a Wraith's night vision was enhanced, but in the inky darkness of this room, even that wouldn't help. At the far end of the room, he could see the golden glow of candlelight illuminating a single, robed figure.

It looked up as Quinn neared, its yellow eyes glowing ominously in the low light. "Master

Quinn," One boomed in an unnatural voice. "Thank you for accepting our summons."

Quinn stepped past the two High Wraiths and dropped to his knee. "It is my honor to stand before you."

One chuckled softly and instructed Quinn to rise. "There is no need for ceremony now, my friend. We have more pressing matters at hand."

Quinn nodded and stood. "Where are the other members of the council?"

"They have been called away on emergency matters." It quickly changed the topic to its own will. "We have a new assignment for you," One began slowly. Moving toward Quinn, it reached out and placed a hand on his shoulder. "This is of the utmost importance."

"How can I serve?"

One stared deeply into Quinn's eyes searching. The elder council member wasn't sure the correct Wraith had been chosen for this duty, but one look into Quinn's face absolved any concerns that had been lingering. "This assignment is completely voluntary," One stated portentously.

"I understand." Quinn nodded.

"Our operatives in Southern France and Italy have reported some disturbing news," One said slowly. "It seems that the two Vampire Lords who controlled that area, Krath and Stephanov, have been assassinated."

Quinn let the news sink in for a moment as he reflected on the possible ramifications. "There will be a struggle for power in the vacuum." He took a long breath. "A vampire war?"

One nodded its head. "It has already begun. We understand that a new vampire has stepped in and gathered many of Krath and Stephanov's men under his new banner. He is waging all-out war on the other clans in Europe, and with the size of his army, we have little doubt that his campaign will be successful. If this is allowed to continue, the vampires of Europe will be united and any advantage we had will be gone. Our strategies rely on the fact that the Lords maintain control of their respective territories. We want them to continue fighting among each other, keeping the lines of communication broken. I fear that if the vampire clans are united, the Wraith will be their first target."

"Who is this new lord?" Quinn asked, his concern obvious.

"We do not know," One breathed. "Our spies were unable to identify him."

Quinn felt a sinking feeling in his gut. "And that's where I come in?"

One paused, then nodded slowly. "We want you to infiltrate this new lord's ranks and learn his identity."

"And report back?"

One nodded again. "If the opportunity to destroy this creature arises, do not hesitate to take it. Otherwise, learn all you can and report back. This is not a suicide mission," One assured him, "but it will be difficult. We have already lost three Wraiths to this new lord and his men. I do not want to add your name to that list."

Quinn took a long breath. Lifting his head, he

stared off into the darkness as he considered the proposition before him. "I would like to make one request."

One waited patiently, allowing the Master Wraith to speak.

"I want Emily St. Louise to accompany me."

One shook its head. "I cannot allow that."

"Why?" Quinn asked, trying not to sound disappointed.

"She is needed elsewhere," One said quickly. "Her destiny does not lead down the same path you currently tread."

Quinn nodded solemnly. There was no point in arguing. Once the council had spoken, their will was set in stone.

"Time is of the essence," One pressed. "I'm afraid I can't give you time to put your affairs in order before you go…" it stopped and reconsidered its words, "should you choose to. I can't stress how important this is—"

Quinn waved off One's continued sales pitch. "I'll go. When do I leave?"

One smiled, obviously pleased with Quinn's response. "Immediately."

CHAPTER FIVE

The multicolored lights of the club flashed and stuttered as the music throbbed. The deep bass sound from the huge speakers resonated off the bodies and glass. The hundreds of people crammed on the dance floor shook and undulated in perfect rhythm. The house DJ, swathed in yellow and black name brand clothes, directed the unholy orgy of flesh and leather like a conductor addressing a symphony. As his fingers worked over the pots of his mixing console, he held one side of his headphones to his ear as he cued up the next track. Ramping up the tempo on the second album, he matched beats of the two songs and slammed the cross fader, seamlessly intermixing the two songs. The layers of hard bodies responded to the new track, grinding harder and faster.

The club, deep in the belly of Berlin, Germany, was a nightmare of chains, girders, and raw metal. An angry web of steel rods, pipes, and glass made up the floor and walls. Chains were draped over the corners and hung from the ceiling ominously. The bar, made from heavy iron girders, stretched across the entire side of the club and was scattered with glasses of every shape and color. Giant plasma screens mounted in the walls, each showing graphic images of war and sex, were intermixed with heavy metal and industrial videos. A grinder, high above the dance floor, continuously cut into beams of metal sending golden showers of sparks cascading down through the glass walls. Huge fog machines, cooled by specially designed devices, spewed white fog along the ground. The thick, noxious chemical crawled along the floors and walls, hiding a multitude of sins. It was a techno-industrial palace, a shrine to everything these people clung to.

Though imperceptible, they were there. Mixed in with the crowd, they moved around and past the humans completely unnoticed on their nightly hunt. Golden eyes were hidden behind masks of thought, fangs concealed by a haze of illusion. They were vampires searching for the kill—some, for the sustenance, others, for the sheer adrenaline. In a club of this size, packed to capacity as it was, there would be no problem culling one of the cattle from the herd and bleeding them dry. They were modern predators and this was their element, their steel jungle. Everything was perfect here—the house lights were low, while bursts of colored lights temporarily confused the crowd's senses, and odds were, if one of these people disappeared, no one would even miss them.

Clad in their camouflage of black leather and flesh, the vampires made their way through the crowd. As the house and party lights dropped at systematic times during the DJ's mix, the first vampire struck. Running his fingers over his bald, tattooed scalp, he adjusted his sunglasses and locked in on his target. Wading easily though the shoulder-to-shoulder crowd, he stopped just behind a young nineteen year old girl and watched as she twisted and dipped her body to the rhythm as if she were in a trance. Her stunning body was barely hidden behind a skintight bra of red latex, a black leather miniskirt, and six inch stiletto fuck-me heels. Her outfit left little to the imagination—nor did the fact she had no visible panty line. A fine layer of sweat covered her perfect body and hair, causing her to glisten in the lights. Standing no less than three feet away, the vampire became enthralled by her blond hair as she shook and tossed it around her head. It was almost a shame to waste this beautiful creature for food, the vampire thought for a moment.

In a swirl of black leather, the vampire was next to her. Edging out the woman's dancing companion, the vampire began to mimic her dance. The woman smiled and laughed as her new partner moved in sync with her. The beat slowed, allowing the powerful bass line to wash over the two. As she looked into the vampire's green eyes just above his smoky glasses, the two were suddenly alone. Wrapping her slender arms around the vampire's neck, the young woman's smile was replaced by intense desire. Pushing her body close, she spun and rubbed her hips against his crotch. Throwing her hair back, it fell over the vampire's shoulder as she pressed her back to his chest. Running his almost porcelain white hands down over her shoulders and to her sides, the woman felt a buzz run down her spine. Moments before, she had been happily dancing with her friend, now she wanted this man more than she could even fathom. Spinning quickly in his arms, she pressed her breasts to his chest and crossed her legs over entwining his. Taking a deep breath, she could practically taste him. As the two continued to dance and grind against each other, the music intensified and quickened. Pumping harder and faster, the woman tried not to lose control.

The vampire slowly leaned in and kissed her on the neck. "Do you want me?" he asked in German.

The young woman moaned as she ran her hands over his cool, bald scalp. "God, yes."

The vampire smiled.

Pushing her from the dance floor, the two hit the wall just as a shower of sparks fell down around them. Groping, rubbing, and exploring, the two dancers were all over each other in an instant. Leaning in, the vampire ran his lips over the woman's fragile throat. Cocking his head slightly, he opened his mouth, exposing the glistening fangs for the first time. Dragging the tips lightly over her flesh, he waited for a response. Only a soft moan could be heard. Taking in the woman's scent, the vampire could wait no longer. He could hear the blood rushing just beneath the woman's skin as her heart pumped hard with excitement. Finding the major artery in her neck with the ease of experience, he dug his fangs in. The woman gasped once but the sensation of pain quickly faded. Holding the vampire tighter in her arms, she was in rapture. Swallowing down a quick gulp of air, she felt her vision begin to blur.

The vampire felt a hand clamp on his shoulder. Spinning around, the woman still firmly in his arms with blood running down her throat, he flashed his golden eyes and hissed to warn off any other who might think of claiming his catch for their own. His eyes suddenly widened. Dropping the woman, he took an uneasy step back. "What the fuck?"

Standing before him was Bane, the slits of his metal faceplate glowing ominously. Draped in black, two long, curved silver blades extended almost two feet from each arm. Bringing the blades up and across his chest, Bane bowed slightly to the other vampire, his hood and mask hiding any trace of the creature beneath. "You have a choice," his deep voice crackled, "join me, or die."

The bald vampire took another step back trying to get out of Bane's extended reach. "What the shit is wrong with you?" The vampire stared angrily at the cloaked figure before him. "This is Groban territory. You have no authority here. So take your melodramatic ass outside."

"I see you have made your decision," Bane cackled. Bane smiled, although the other vampire couldn't tell, pleased that he hadn't given up. He was in the mood for a fight. "This is my territory now."

The vampire lunged. "You son of a—"

Bane's opponent was dead before his feet left the ground. Whipping his arm blades out and down, Bane easily excised the vampire's head. As the body hit the floor at his feet, he stepped back to avoid the blue flames as they slung red embers into the air.

Kicking the charred corpse aside, Bane spun to face the crowd. Several of the other Groban Clan vampires had seen the attack and were advancing on him. Lifting his hand, Bane snapped his fingers once. A hail of gunfire instantly filled the room from all sides, the sharp sound sliced through the thrum of the speakers. As the bullets tore into vampires and humans alike, Bane went on the offensive. Using his mental camouflage to cloak himself, he easily disappeared into the crowd. As one of the Groban vampires went down in a flurry of bullets, the creature suddenly felt the cold slice of steel through his heart. Looking up, he saw Bane materialize like a ghost, with his arm blade buried deep into his torso. Drawing the blade back, Bane cleaved the vampire in two. As the creature's shrieks filled the air, Bane's vampires advanced.

Each a refugee from a fallen clan, they had branded themselves with dark, tribal tattoos down the left side of their faces to show their new allegiance. As the first vampire made it down the steps into the club, he was knocked to the ground by one from the Groban Clan and decapitated. Drawing the automatic weapons around, the remaining Bane Vamps lit into the attacker. His body convulsed and was thrown back as several clips were emptied into him. Writhing on the ground, he roared in pain but knew the bullets would not kill him. They just hurt like hell. As he started to lift himself out of the pool of blood that had gathered around him, a Bane Vamp was on him. With a flash of steel as the vampire pulled a knife, the one from the Groban Clan fell back to the ground dead. As his body was engulfed in flame, the Bane Vamp ripped his knife from the dead vampire's heart and stood up. Turning back into the club, he lifted his weapon and continued the assault.

As the crowd screamed and tried to break free of the war zone that had erupted, bullets hit innocent men and women, dropping them to the ground. Chaos ruled the moment as Groban and Bane's Vampires met in the center of the dance floor. As clips were emptied, weapons were abandoned in favor of melee attacks. Vampires clawed, cut, sliced, and chopped their way through each other, creating an inferno of blue fire that chewed through the club. Wave after wave of Bane's Vamps threw themselves into the fray, easily outnumbering Groban's.

As Bane looked on from his perch above the bar, he wiped the blood on his blades off with his heavy cape. This clan was inconsequential to his plan. There was no need for recruitment, just total obliteration. Groban was nothing more than a virus in this part of Germany and Bane cared little for his actual territory, but resistance was a possibility. There was no other choice but to wipe this clan from the continent if he were to rule completely. It was of no matter. Tonight's stop was little more than a stress reliever for his men. Those who survived could have their way with the remaining humans.

As his army swept across Europe, there was only one thing which could possibly stand in his way—the Gwyliad Wriaeth. They would have to be dealt with quickly. Bane gritted his teeth. He didn't have time for their nonsense. His attack must be a bolt from the blue and utterly devastating. To wipe out one academy would do little more than enrage his hunters. He would have to attack on multiple fronts, eliminating all Wraiths at once. Laughing to himself, he thought of their schools and strongholds burning. It would be glorious.

Lifting his arm blades to the side, he looked like a vulture poised for the attack. Staring down into the battle below, he spied several of Groban's vampires surrounded by his own. Leaping high into the air, he came down in the center of the three, sending shards of glass and steel from the floor careening into the air. As the debris still hung in the air, he rammed his blade into the back of the first vampire and lifted him off the ground. Slinging him around into the next one, Bane pulled the blade free, and with a scissor motion, clipped through the two creatures. Whipping his bloody blades around, he dug them deep into the sides of the third vampire. Pressing forward, he pushed the blades all the way up into the vampire's chest until his fists were pinned against its back. Flexing his muscles, Bane tore the blades sideways, shredding the Groban vampire. Lifting his head up, he roared in enjoyment. Spinning around, he charged back into the battle.

***

The warm morning sun filtered in through her window, warming her naked body. Rolling from her side onto her back, Saint yawned and stretched her arms above her head. Her eyes still closed, she reached across her small bed. Finding only sheets, she slowly began to wake. Opening her eyes, she found the empty spot where Miller had been. Slowly sitting up, a quick moment of sadness hit her. After last night's escapades, she had hoped to wake up and cuddle in his arms. Rubbing the heel of her hand over her face, she let her dark hair fall forward. He must've left sometime early in the morning. Standing, Saint grabbed her dark blue robe off a nearby chair and pulled it on. As she walked across her small room toward the door, she stopped and smiled. Miller had left a note after all. Glancing into her mirror, she saw a heart drawn in red lipstick with Miller's name signed below it. Unfortunately, he had ruined her favorite tube, but it was the thought that counted...right?

She grumbled once under her breath as she lifted the tube. The sharp edge she had been working so diligently to create had been completely destroyed. Shrugging her shoulders, she tossed it in a nearby trash bin and resumed her trek to the bathroom. Lifting her towel off a hook, she slung it over her shoulder and pulled open her door. Stepping outside, applause erupted. Looking up with a start, Saint saw that nearly every girl in the dorm was present. Each dressed in their pajamas, robes and slippers, they continued to clap, whistle and cheer for Saint.

Saint looked to the nearest girl, her dorm neighbor, Jasmine. "What's all this then?"

Jasmine smiled and laughed. "The performance you gave last night was incredible."

Saint blushed and covered her mouth with her hand.

"Everyone in the dorm could hear you and Miller," Jasmine continued. "Especially you."

"Oh my god," Saint breathed, "I didn't know we were being that loud." Embarrassed, she tried to slink back into her room.

"Oh no you don't." Jasmine, a tall black girl with blond streaks through her curly hair, reached out and grabbed Saint by the arm. "You don't get off that easy."

Saint shook her head and reached for the doorknob.

Jasmine pulled her along. "Come on."

Saint could easily overpower the student Wraith, but chose not to. Jasmine had just returned back from her five year tour of duty, but was deemed unready for the ritual. A dark scar ran horizontally along her cheek to the right corner of her mouth. Jasmine hadn't told the story of how she had received it, but Saint knew it was a lesson she wouldn't have to learn twice. The council had assigned her an additional year of study. More than likely, with a large graduating class this year, the council had to be really selective when choosing the seven participants in the ritual. Saint was just glad she didn't have to wait. She and Jasmine had been next-door neighbors since they had entered the academy. Although never truly close friends, each had spent more than a few evenings in the other's room talking. It had given Saint the chance to, among other things, be a girl every once and a while. In this male-dominated lifestyle she had chosen, it was easy to forget sometimes.

As the other girls began to disperse, Jasmine pulled Saint toward her room. Pushing open the door, she pulled Saint inside. Leaning against the door to close it, Jasmine leered at Saint oddly. "You don't look any different."

"Am I supposed to?" Saint countered.

"I don't know," Jasmine answered after a moment. "I'm just not sure what I expected. You are the first Wraith I've known before and after the ritual." She moved further into the room and sat down on the edge of her bed. "What was it like?"

"Candles, blood, sacred knives," Saint said nonchalantly. "You know, ritual stuff."

"No," Jasmine shook her head, "what did it feel like?"

"I can't," Saint paused, "I don't know how to describe it properly." She bit her bottom lip. "It was like nothing else I've ever experienced."

"That doesn't help much." Jasmine laughed. "Do you feel different now?"

Saint shook her head. "I don't want to disappoint you, but not really. I mean, I know I'm stronger, faster, and have all the enhanced senses now, but I'm still just me."

"Except for those," Jasmine said, pointing to Saint's mouth. "I don't think those are standard issue."

Saint quickly closed her mouth, almost ashamed of her fangs. "I don't know how I got these. Master Quinn was very concerned at first."

"I don't know." She laughed. "I think they look cool. Makes you look dangerous."

Saint smiled. "They creep me out."

"So, you and Miller are back together again?" she asked, changing the subject away from what was obviously bothering Saint.

Saint turned and sat down in a chair opposite Jasmine. "No."

"No? After the opera we heard from your room

last night?"

"We were just saying goodbye," Saint admitted to both Jasmine and herself. "It was one last fling."

Jasmine was slightly taken aback by Saint's honesty. "Is something happening?" Her mood changed from perky to concerned.

"You've heard about those stories of solders telling their loved ones that tomorrow they ship off to war and may never come back, right?"

Jasmine nodded.

"Same thing." Saint shrugged.

"You can't really believe that."

"Why shouldn't I? The average life span for a Wraith isn't that long."

"Oh my god, girl, what is this funk you've slipped into?" Jasmine stood up and walked toward Saint. "We need to get some chocolate in you."

Saint laughed softly.

"What's really the matter?" Jasmine asked as she knelt down in front of her friend.

"I just," Saint shook her head and took a breath, "I've been thinking about death a lot lately."

"Why?"

"I can't really say. It could be the whole commencement thing, but Miller brought it up last night, too," she said with a wave of her hand. "Probably that I'm due for my first solo assignment isn't helping."

"You think you're going out there on your own and will get killed on your first mission?"

"The odds are good," Saint said gloomily.

"Don't give me that crap," Jasmine barked. "You're a damned good Wraith."

Saint shook her head. "But training can only go so far. What if I get out there and make a mistake?"

"What if you walk out the door tomorrow and get hit by a bus?" Jasmine countered. "It can happen, you just have to not think about it. We're all here to fight the good fight, right?"

Saint nodded reluctantly.

Jasmine placed her hand gently on Saint's knee. "Then that's all we can do. You have to stop focusing on death so much. That isn't the Saint I know."

"Who is the Saint you know?"

Jasmine smiled sweetly. "She's a beautiful young woman full of life, who can brighten any room she walks in to."

"Thanks, Jasmine," Saint breathed, "but I stink. I really need to hit the shower."

Jasmine laughed. "I wasn't going to say anything, but damn, girlfriend, you are a little ripe."

"Sleep stink," Saint offered.

"I don't think so honey," Jasmine chuckled, "more like sweaty-rolling-in-the-sheets-all-night-with-Miller stink."

Saint and Jasmine stood and hugged. Patting her friend on the back, Saint slowly withdrew.

"So is it true what they say?" Jasmine asked.

Saint cocked her head slightly. "What's that, Jasmine?"

"Nine inches?"

Saint placed her hand on her forehead and slowly pulled it down her face. "I don't keep a ruler on the nightstand...pervert."

Turning, she headed for the door, hoping this

time to actually make it to the shower. Adjusting her towel, she stepped outside and let out an audible sigh of relief at the empty hall. Letting out a soft laugh at Jasmine's question, she ran her fingertips along the wall. Quickening her pace, she started down the carpeted floor towel in hand. If she could only make it around the corner—

"Saint?"

She let her head fall forward in defeat. Spinning on her heels, she came face-to-face with a High Wraith. "Crap," she muttered under her breath.

"Did I catch you on your way to the shower?"

Saint nodded.

"I'm sorry," the High Wraith apologized, "but the council needs to see you immediately."

"Can I clean up a bit?"

The Wraith shook his head. "Time is short."

"Should I at least put on some clothes?" she asked with a sigh.

The High Wraith glanced down at her shabby bathrobe. "That would probably be appropriate." Turning, he began to walk away. Stopping, he spun on his heels and turned back. "Oh, and, Saint?"

Saint stopped just shy of her dorm. "Yes?"

The High Wraith smiled deviously. "We had a few reports of strange shrieks and loud moans in this part of the compound last night. Didn't happen to see any wild animals going at it around here, did you?"

Saint shook her head innocently.

The High Wraith nodded. "That's what I thought. You do know that there are no boys allowed in the women's dorms, right?"

Saint hung her head as she reached for the doorknob. She couldn't get the door open fast enough to hide her embarrassment.

CHAPTER SIX

She had lost all concept of time. Strapped to a table in a barren room with no windows, she couldn't even tell if it was day or night. Lifting her head, she glanced down. Two thick chains firmly soldered to the edges of the stainless steel table crossed her chest. Additional chains were also wrapped around her wrists and legs securely binding her in place. There was no chance, even at full strength, she could break free.

She caught sight of her left leg and cringed. A new appendage had been attached to her just below the knee. With a completely different build and color than the opposite one, the leg wasn't even close to a match. It looked as if the surgeon had taken the leg from a healthy human instead of another vampire. Her gray, decomposing flesh was a striking difference from the pale, pink flesh of the new leg. Scabs had welled up around the hasty stitching job that bound the leg to her. Trying to wiggle her toes, she found she could feel the leg, but not yet command it. Letting her head fall back onto the table, she knew the leg would soon be fine. Her vampiric chemistry would firmly attach the new appendage and it would begin to decay to match, while her mental projection would hide any sign of it.

The room held no trace of its purpose. It was completely bare and sanitized. Tile floors led into featureless white walls and light gray ceilings. Large banks of fluorescent lights were installed in the roof washing the room in their green hued light.

It was completely emotionless, barren. Although she couldn't see it, she could feel it. She was being watched. The almost imperceptible buzzing of the electronics of the cameras gave it away.

Brigitte struggled vainly at her bonds. Balling her fists, she exerted all her strength pulling against the chains. Her muscles and bones popped and crackled in protest as the chains began to dig into the flesh of her wrists. Falling back with a sigh, she closed her golden eyes for a moment. Focusing her mind, she recovered her mental projection. Her gray flesh faded away to be replaced with healthy pink. The same green cotton dress she had been wearing when she urged Stephanov to attend the peace meeting formed over her body. If she were to die here, she would at least do so with some dignity.

Just then, she heard the click of the doorknob as it was unlocked and twisted open. Lifting her head as high as it could go, she saw two leather-clad vampires with dark tribal tattoos down the sides of their faces slide into the room. As they took positions on either side of the door, a spark of recognition hit Brigitte. Formerly one of Stephanov's men, the vampire standing to the left had been a loyal servant. He had accompanied her on several tasks for their former lord. They had become friends during these times and he was even at her side when Stephanov was killed. She thought he was dead like the others. She caught the vampire's eye and cast him a pleading glance. Without acknowledgment, without emotion, he turned and stared blankly into the room, ignoring her. Brigitte felt her heart sink.

Through the darkness behind the door, a whirl of black cloth erupted. Marching into the room the same way Brigitte had seen him do on the battlefield where her master died, Bane stopped in front of her and focused his burning golden eyes on her. Reaching his gloved hand down, he placed it tenderly on her arm. Brigitte tried to retreat, but there was nowhere to go. Rage welled up inside her at his touch. He had killed her lord, her creator, in a most cowardly manner.

"Don't touch me," she hissed.

"I mean you no harm," his unnatural voice boomed. It almost sounded metallic, but maybe that was Brigitte's perception because of the mask. "I'm here to free you."

"There is nothing you can offer me," Brigitte growled angrily. "You are a coward hiding behind bombs and masks, afraid to dirty your hands."

Bane recoiled slightly at the sheer venom spewing from this beautiful woman's mouth. "Many braver than you have spoken similar words," Bane cautioned, "and they serve me now." He turned and glanced at Stephanov's vampire knowingly.

"Who are you?" Brigitte asked, "I mean behind the mask?"

"Inconsequential," Bane replied quickly. "That vampire is long dead. I am Bane now."

Brigitte laughed out loud at his name. "Bane? Is that the best you've got?" she asked mockingly. "Hey, Darth Vader called, he wants his look back." Brigitte cackled with glee.

Bane's eyes hardened for a moment. "You

mock what you do not understand with your feeble mind." Snapping his hand up, he clamped it around the woman's throat. Leaning close, he stared directly into her eyes. "I am not your enemy."

Brigitte struggled against his iron grip. She felt at any moment, her windpipe would collapse under the pressure he was exerting. "You're not doing a very good job of convincing me," she croaked.

Bane pulled his hand away, unnerved that he had lost his composure so easily. Brushing a lock of hair from her forehead, he ran his fingers down the side of her face to her cheek. "I can see into your soul, Brigitte. I know you want the same thing I do—peace among the vampire nation."

Brigitte heard his voice echo in her ears. She began to feel as if she were looking and listening to him through a tunnel. Even the pain in her leg began to fade. "We need peace," she answered almost robotically as if the words were not her own.

"Indeed," he spoke softly, "I can bring that to the vampires of Europe. We can be whole again."

"We can be whole again," she mimicked.

Bane snapped his fingers and the Stephanov vampire was immediately at his side. Reaching into his leather coat, the vampire handed his lord what looked like an unlabeled wine bottle. Its green colored glass held a dark fluid inside. Taking the bottle into his hands, Bane popped out the cork with a squeak. "All you have to do is drink," he said to Brigitte, "drink, and be with me." Sliding his left hand under her head, he held the bottle at the ready. "Are you with me?"

"I am yours," she mumbled.

Pressing the bottle to her lips, he quickly tipped it back and poured the dark liquid into her open mouth. Corking the bottle, he handed it back to the vampire and waited. Brigitte closed her eyes and swallowed hard, taking the entire mouthful all at once. Her body almost instantly relaxed. Looking up through blurred vision, she stared at Bane's unemotional mask. As the darkness encroached on her vision, her eyes closed again as her head fell back to the table. Bane watched with pleasure as a dark tattoo appeared in her mental projection. The thin, dark lines swirled and twisted beautifully down from below the outward corner of her left eye terminating just above her jawline.

***

She lifted her arm slightly and sniffed her armpit. Leaning back in her seat, she relaxed a bit knowing she didn't outright stink. Running her fingertips over her head, she tried to catch a few of the fly-aways that were defying the ponytail her hair was pulled into. Tugging down her black baby doll t-shirt a bit, she looked down at the chunky pair of black combat boots on her feet. They weren't her favorite and they were hell to fight in, but they were the closest pair in the closet as she scrambled to get dressed. She ran her hands over the low-cut black leather pants she wore for a moment, enjoying their smoothness. They had been left over from a night at the clubs in London a few weeks ago. It was the best she could do on short notice. Hell, she felt lucky to be fully dressed at this point instead of in her bathrobe.

Saint rubbed her eyes with the heels of her palms to try and wipe away some of the sleep. Tilting her head back, she yawned deeply. As she closed her mouth, she squeaked as she bit her lip with her new fangs. Quickly yanking her fingertips to her bottom lip, she drew away a small bead of blood. Shaking her head with a slight grimace, she hoped she would get used to her new teeth soon. She wondered for a moment about getting them filed down, but reconsidered. She didn't think the Gwyliad Wriaeth offered dental insurance.

With a smirk, she stood and looked around the small waiting area outside the council chambers. Two small benches, much like the one she was seated on, and several tall, potted plants littered the area. The same tan walls that dominated the architecture of the rest of the Academy were present here as well. Two long banners, hanging from the ceiling and almost touching the floor, were positioned against the wall opposite the main doors. They were constructed of red silk with black borders. Black, hand-stitched symbols ran vertically down the banners in a language Saint didn't recognize. For all she knew, they could easily have been Klingon instead of some ancient, lost dialect.

Leaning against a nearby wall with her hands tucked behind her back, she stared at the banners. The letters seemed to come alive and dance against the shimmering red background. As she continued to stare, she found herself suddenly lost in a sea of red, shimmering silk. The thick, black letters whipped and twirled around her head. She found herself transfixed by them. Their meaning, much like a word lost on the tip of her tongue, seemed familiar, yet just out of reach. She strained her mind for comprehension, searching every memory, every hidden bit of data. Suddenly, as if hit by some unseen blast, recognition struck her. Opening her pale blue eyes wide, the once-foreign letters were now inexplicably understandable.

She snapped herself out of her daze and charged toward the banners. Running her fingers over the silk fabric, she translated aloud. "We are those," she jumped to the second banner, "who are to blame." She took a deep breath and stepped back, realizing it was an ancient vampire dialect. Cocking her head to the right, she struggled to understand the cryptic message. Her mind snapped back to the conversation she and Master Quinn were having in her dorm. He mentioned something very similar about the Wraith, but had been interrupted. She had to find him. She had to know what this meant, and more importantly, how she knew it.

Turning, she took one step and stopped, remembering where she was. The small hairs on the back of her neck stood up. Craning her head around, she felt a pair of eyes burning into her. Spinning on her heels, she saw the unblinking golden eyes set deep within the darkened hood of a white robe. A sudden pang of guilt erupted in her stomach as the figure melted back into the darkness of the council chamber. Saint took a step forward, but stopped herself. To charge into the council without permission and escort meant instant death for anyone, including students.

Dropping quickly back into her seat, she closed her eyes and pressed her fingertips to her temples. As she messaged them lightly, she drew a long, slow breath trying to calm the ball of rattlesnakes that seethed and writhed in her guts. She knew the council member had been standing there long enough to see her translate the banners. She wasn't meant to read them. No student was. She understood that now. More words from her mentor surfaced, vampires have genetic memories. She cursed under her breath again. Apparently, she had inherited more than just the fangs.

"Acolyte Wraith St. Louise?"

Saint looked up with a start to see a High Wraith standing to her right. His face was blank and emotionless. Saint shrank away from him slightly, guilt settling on her face. Her fingertips started to tingle, signaling their readiness to go numb at any moment. He could just as easily kill her on the spot as lead her into the council chambers. She drew a sharp breath. "Yes?"

He stared at her with unwavering eyes. "The council has requested your presence."

Standing, Saint's legs felt weak below her. She nodded to the maroon-vested Wraith. Reaching out, she steadied herself against the wall for a moment as she took another breath.

"Are you all right?" the High Wraith inquired.

Saint nodded and forced a smile. "Just feeling a bit lightheaded there for a minute. I'm okay now." Adjusting her black baby doll t-shirt to cover a bit more of her midriff, she then brushed a lock of hair out of her face. Turning, she addressed the High Wraith. "I'm ready."

The High Wraith opened the double doors of the darkened room and motioned for her to go inside.

"You're not coming with?"

The High Wraith shook his head. "My instructions were just to let you inside, not to escort you."

The knot in her stomach welled up again. She was dead. She knew it. Looking from the High Wraith into the darkened room, she balled her fists. If she was to die here, she would do it with dignity. Nodding to the High Wraith, she stepped into the darkness. Immediately, the large doors were slammed shut behind her. Her instincts screamed for her to turn and tear down the doors, but she fought them. With her new strength, she could easily rip the mighty doors from their hinges, but the High Wraith on the other side would probably dispatch her, or at least slow her down enough so that others could capture her. The darkness of the room engulfed her. Feeling as if she were about to drown in it, she tried to steady her nerves. Letting her eyes adjust for a moment, she tried to make out any details of the chamber. She could barely discern a set of stairs at the far side of the room and several rectangular columns that supported the roof, but little else.

Swallowing hard, she aligned herself with what she hoped was the front of the room. Taking her first tentative step, she heard the thick sole of her boot echo through the inky blackness. Pressing ahead, she saw a single candle flicker to life in the center of the room. Stopping, she watched as others lit, marking a clear path to the front. As more and more candles came to life, the room was awash in a flickering, golden light. Saint noticed the seven members of the council standing together at the front of the room for the first time, each with their back to her. Moving ahead, she stopped a few feet short of the main steps that led up to the council's platform. It was raised above the floor by a mesh of black ironwork and stone.

"Acolyte Wraith Emily St. Louise," One's voice boomed.

Saint looked up, instantly recognizing the voice. It was the head of the order, her creator, speaking to her now. "Yes?"

The seven slowly turned to face her, their yellow eyes burning in the low light. "Since the ritual, you have displayed some disturbing traits." One took a step toward her.

Saint felt her heart sink into her chest. She was about to die. She said nothing.

"This has concerned the council greatly," Four added.

"Greatly," the others echoed.

One held up a hand to silence the other six members of the Esgobaeth. It looked straight at Saint with obvious curiosity on its face. "How do you feel?"

Saint was taken aback by the question. Looking directly at One, a million responses ran through her mind. "I feel," she breathed, "fine." She gritted her teeth at the reply. It was probably the most inane thing she could come up with.

"Fine?" One echoed. "Please elaborate."

"I don't understand the question," Saint said in exasperation.

One walked slowly down the steps and stopped in front of her. Reaching out its hand, One placed it tenderly on her shoulder. "Don't fear us, child," it said calmly. "We just want to understand. No Wraith has ever received the virus the way you have."

Saint shook her head, although its words did comfort her slightly. "I still don't understand."

One smiled softly, exposing its fangs. "For each, the virus is different. For some, the strength is diminished. Others develop a slight aversion to sunlight, even though it cannot hurt them. Still others develop keen senses and no other abilities. You however," One looked over the young wraith, "seem to be a perfect blend."

"Of what?" Saint asked, slightly more confident.

One laughed. "Vampire and human, of course."

Saint instantly knew it to be true.

"You have all of their strengths, and none of their weaknesses," One stopped, "we hope."

Saint cocked her head slightly. "What do you mean, we hope?"

"Long ago, there was a man named Gwynn Ap Nudd," One stated. Taking a step back, it sat down on the first step. Patting the step with its hand, One motioned for Saint to do the same. As she sat down next to it, One patted her gently on the back. "He was the progenitor of the Gwyliad Wriaeth," One said proudly. "Born a Celt, he lived his life well by their standards. A natural hunter, he excelled in providing his village with fresh meat and the skins they required to make clothes and shelters. He was very successful until a band of vampires attacked and killed every man, woman and child in his village."

"So vampires have been around just as long as the Wraith?"

One shook its head. "Longer. It wasn't until much later when science and medicine advanced enough that we discovered vampirism is nothing more than a transmittable virus."

"Vampirism is an STD." Saint chuckled. "Makes sense."

One nodded. "It is blood-borne, and when introduced into a human host, its effects are devastating. But I'm getting ahead of myself," One breathed, "back to my story."

Saint nodded.

"Gwynn vowed to find the creatures that killed his people and exact his revenge. Donning a gray cloak and riding a white steed, he did it the only way he knew how—he hunted them relentlessly. Using a common farming scythe, he fought his way valiantly through the vampires, but their numbers were too great. He was attacked," One paused, "and bitten."

Saint gasped, enraptured by the story. "He contracted the virus?"

One nodded. "The virus attacks the human body differently in each case. For most, it kills them nearly instantly, but for others, it takes root

101

and changes the host into a new vampire. Current theories hold that Gwynn fell into a third, extremely rare category. He was born with a unique body chemistry, which when introduced to the vampirism virus, mutated it. He gained all of their power and none of their weaknesses," he essayed. "He had no blood lust, would not burn in the sun, and did not take on the appearance of those wretched beasts."

"So vampires back then looked the same?"

One nodded. "More or less. They were horrid creatures with yellow eyes, fangs, and claws. Their bodies were gray and pale as their flesh rotted away when they hadn't fed enough. But they could not appear in human form, nor did they have enhanced strength or speed."

"I don't understand."

One pointed toward the main doors. "What did the banners say outside?"

Saint paused, unsure if her answer would damn her. Taking a deep breath, she recited the message, "We are those who are to blame."

"Remember that," One said quickly. "We'll get back to it." It adjusted itself on the step and continued. "Gwynn found that he could pass on this gift through his blood. He then realized the magnitude of his powers and set out to create the White Guard, the Gwyliad Wriaeth. In short order, he had created hundreds of Guardsman—as they were known back then—to fight off the vampires. They rode magnificently into battle," One smiled, imagining the scene in its mind, "and nearly had the vampires wiped out."

"What happened?" Saint asked the obvious

question.

"A Guardsman betrayed the order," One said gravely. "This man, Arawn, wanted to use his new powers for more than just extermination, he wanted to rule. Created by the very hand of Gwynn, he turned his back on the Guard and went willingly into the hands of our enemy. He made a pact with the largest remaining vampire clan to use them as his army in exchange for their continued free reign over the lands. To his surprise, the clan agreed and Arawn built a mighty army to oppose the Gwyliad Wriaeth very quickly." One paused, obviously disturbed by the story he was recounting. "Shortly after several staggering defeats at the hands of the Guard, Arawn's creatures turned on him. When the vampire virus, along with the one of the mutated Wraith, met in his body, it created a new super virus we've now dubbed 'Necolamia Morbus'— Vampire Death Disease. Arawn was now nearly immortal with all the strength and power of the Guard, but the necessity for blood remained. He also inherited the horrid form of the creatures, but found that he could alter his appearance in the minds of those who looked at him. Arawn was the source of the new breed of vampires." One took a deep breath. "So in essence, vampires created the Gwyliad Wriaeth, and the Gwyliad Wriaeth created the vampires we know today. We are those who are to blame."

Saint sat back, stunned at the story she had just heard. "Why are you telling me this? Isn't this a forbidden subject?"

"It is," One smiled, "but we thought you should

know. We think you share the same type of unique body chemistry Gwynn had."

Saint quickly put two and two together. "My body is mutating the Wraith Virus?"

One nodded. "We believe so. You may be the first of a completely new breed of Wraith."

"Wicked." Saint smiled.

"Indeed." One smiled. "I'm sure a few tests will confirm our theories."

"Wait, whoa," Saint said quickly, "tests? I thought I was done with tests now that I've graduated."

"I don't think you understand your importance to this order," One said quickly. "Your unique body will give us insight into how we were created! We will finally be able to prove our theories on the origin of the Gwyliad Wriaeth."

"Do I have a choice in the matter?"

One shook its head. "Not really, no."

She bit her lip. "Don't do this. Please." Her voice was soft and quiet.

One stared at her unblinking. The corners of One's mouth started to sag down into a frown, but it quickly caught itself. One had been watching this girl since her entrance into the academy. She was their brightest pupil and yet her future had been decided here tonight. "I have to. If you are let out into the field and happen to fall into vampire hands, the consequences could be devastating. We could be looking at a whole new breed of vampire if that happens. This cannot be allowed."

"What if I run?" Saint said with a smirk.

"There are ten High Wraiths in this room right

now. You might take one or two," One estimated, his tone turning dark, "but they will bring you down." He placed his hand on her shoulder. "Don't run, child."

Saint turned and looked into the room. She could just make out the silhouettes of the High Wraiths standing guard. He was right. If she ran, she wouldn't even make it to the door. Turning back to One, she nodded solemnly. "I won't run."

One nodded. Several High Wraiths appeared out of the darkness and took Saint into custody. Turning her away from the council, they started toward the doors. Glancing back over her shoulder, Saint shot one last pleading glance at the council. With a stern face, One demonstrated there would no reprieve. Dropping her head down, she exited the council chambers silently.

***

Quinn stopped. Holding his breath, he spun and pressed his back to the wall. Flattening out his body as much as he could, he listened to the click of booted feet in the adjacent hall. As he inched toward the corner, he caught a whiff of one of the men's cologne. It was the same. Poking his head around, he peered up the hallway. Satisfied that it was empty, he ducked out and moved briskly following the scent of cologne. He knew these were the same vampires he had been tracking all night. Their scent was unmistakable. Whipping his tattered coat behind him, he was careful to check each doorway as he passed. With his hand firmly on the pommel of his scythe, he picked up his pace.

Little time had passed since he left the Wraith Academy in England. A fellow Wraith who had witnessed a massacre at a vampire bar in Berlin had tipped Quinn off. His quarry had led him into the heart of France near the town of Saint Malo on the Emerald Coast. Latching onto the group in Germany, he had encountered them just outside Berlin and tracked them here. They each bore tribal tattoos on their faces unlike any Quinn had ever seen before. If his hunch played out, these would be soldiers in this new lord's army. If not, they were still vampires that needed to be dispatched. Either way, he hoped they would lead him to their new lord.

Coming around a corner, he heard voices. Ducking into a nearby room, he perked up his ears to listen. He couldn't make out every word, but they were discussing a raid of some sorts in Paris. From what he understood, this new clan had been working its way through Europe, wiping out one clan after another. As two new voices joined the conversation, he heard mentions of a conquered Italy and forces advancing in Spain. It seemed as if this highly advanced military maneuver was being coordinated all over the continent with similar results. If their pace continued, the vampires would attain what other leaders and dictators had not: A unified Europe. Who was this new Vampire Lord, and how could he instill such confidence and loyalty in his men? Vampires were notoriously fickle when it came to affiliations. They usually did what suited them best and damn the consequences.

Yet this one man was able to control armies all over Europe with little more than an order. Add that to the puzzle, Quinn told himself. Slinking back into the shadows, he disappeared into the mansion.

A pair of golden eyes flashed in the darkness where he had just been standing. Turning, they followed the Wraith into the darkness.

CHAPTER SEVEN

"Where are you taking me? Guys?"

The High Wraiths said nothing as they escorted Saint deeper into the bowels of the academy. Two were holding her arms, while a third shadowed the group for safety. Completely silent since leaving the council's chamber, they had moved her past the bustling classrooms and training rooms, further inside than she had ever been. This place was old, almost ancient. The drab, sterile walls gave way to exposed brick and cobwebs as they walked. The banks of fluorescent lights in the ceiling slowly faded away, leaving only oil lamps flickering against the gloom.

Moving up through the hallway, Saint heard a familiar noise with her enhanced hearing. Straining in the darkness, she heard the faint whirr of electric motors churning. It was the sound of surveillance cameras following the group as it moved. The security around this area was tightening. There was something down here not meant for students. Reaching out into the darkness, she could sense electricity pulsing through thick cables along the floor. It could have been part of some kind of alarm or detection system, but she couldn't see how. There were no motion detectors installed (that she could sense) or weight sensitive plates in the floor. As they rounded the final corner on their journey, Saint finally understood.

Situated in the end of the hall was a small elevator door. A single fluorescent light tube was installed in a channel above the door, casting a sickly, blue-green light into the hallway. The door was constructed of a thick, steel mesh and had to be hand opened. As the High Wraiths slid the first gate to the left, they had to reach down and lift a second mesh gate up. This elevator predated Saint, was maybe even older than the two High Wraiths who stood next to her. Allowing the third High Wraith to step in first, they situated Saint in the center of the rickety wooden floor and took flanking positions on either side of her. Sliding the two gates closed, the High Wraith on Saint's right reached out. For the first time, she noticed the anachronism. A sleek, brushed aluminum keypad was attached to the wall. It's recessed, laser-etched keys had individual blue LED lights beneath them that gave the pad an eerie glow. Tapping in a five-digit code, the four felt the elevator lurch once as the brakes unlocked. As the High Wraith pressed the down arrow on the pad, the elevator groaned and creaked as it started its decent.

Through the mesh fencing, Saint could see banks of crimson lights lining the shaft. She watched as alternating bands of red and darkness lit the stoic High Wraiths' faces, creating a devilish haze. She felt as if she were descending deeper and deeper into the very depths of hell. She began to feel slightly claustrophobic, expecting at any moment to see flames leap up from the floorboards and small, bulbous demons bearing pitchforks to appear and begin torturing her. She was letting her mind run away with her—but the strangeness of the situation wasn't helping. She had expected to be on her first full mission as a Wraith now, not being drug down into Dante's Inferno. She felt a flush of anger in her face. They were taking her life away, taking her dreams.

Looking up, she felt the elevator lurch to a stop. Seconds later, she heard the sound of metal clamping against metal, the brakes locking again, no doubt. Sliding the elevator open, they revealed a polished silver door. Reaching between the elevator and wall, the first High Wraith tapped an invisible button. As the doors cracked open with a hiss of released air, a bright, white light flooded into the elevator. As her eyes adjusted, Saint peered into the hall that looked more at home in a science fiction movie rather than beneath an ancient training facility. There were no details or sharp corners visible on its glistening, white veneer. All edges were smoothly rounded, appearing like the corridor of a spacecraft. With High Wraiths next to and behind her, Saint stepped into the hall. The smell of antiseptic and medical supplies hit her nostrils, making her skin crawl. Two men in light green scrubs emerged from a door at the far end of the hallway. Both wearing surgical masks and smoky goggles, they glanced toward Saint but quickly continued on their way without a hint of interest. Turning to the right, they pressed an unseen panel on the wall, opening another door and vanished inside. Shooting a worried look to the three High Wraiths guarding her, Saint silently pleaded to be let free. She didn't belong here. The sterile, impersonal exterior surely hid a dark secret she didn't want to be a party to.

Stopping at a recessed door, the High Wraiths

touched a panel, activating the door. As it slid open, it revealed a mint green tiled room with silver medical equipment of every shape and size. An examination table sat patiently in the center just below an immense light waiting for its next occupant. Nearby tables were lined with surgical cutting tools and a host of needles and wires. Saint felt her heart sink into her gut as the men led her toward the table. She had the sudden impression of being a school science project that was about to be dissected. Her mouth became dry. It was as if all the moisture in her body was sticking to her palms at the moment. Wiping them against her black shirt, the High Wraiths pushed her toward the table. As they let go, she placed her hands flat on the cool, polished surface.

Saint gritted her teeth. She would not go quietly into the night. She would not.

Throwing herself forward, she maneuvered her body into a perfect handstand on the edge of the table. Kicking with her legs, she vaulted up and spun in midair. Landing on the balls of her feet, she crouched down and faced her three escorts. Witnessing her gymnastic feat, they had already gone on the offensive. The first High Wraith lunged at her. Leaping up, she avoided his hands. Bringing her legs down quickly, she snapped them on either side of his arms and twisted, tying him up. Leaning forward, she wrapped her arm around the back of his neck and leapt off the table. As she hit the ground, her opponent flipped gracefully backwards over her arm and continued his attack. Whipping her head around, Saint dodged the blow just in time to see the second and third members of her escort joining the fray. Weaving in, she balled her fist and hit the first man in the sternum with a crunch. As he fell back, the third High Wraith delivered a heavy right hook across her chin, snapping her head around. Using the momentum of the punch, Saint dropped down, spun, and swept his legs. As the second High Wraith toppled to the ground, her confidence rose. These were the best of the best and she was gaining the upper hand.

Standing quickly, she pressed her attack. Targeting the third man, she launched toward him. Easily intercepting her out of the air, the third High Wraith smashed her head first into the wall. Without giving her a chance to recover, he plucked her from the floor with his preternatural strength and lifted her high above his head. The High Wraith dropped down to one knee and brought Saint crashing down over the other. She grunted in pain as her back crackled in protest. Ignoring the pain, she kicked up hard and connected her knee with his chin. Flipping backward off his knee, she vaulted up and landed flatfooted. Pain surged up her spine.

All three escorts were on their feet again and blocking the door. Never taking their eyes off her, even to blink, the three High Wraiths charged in perfect rhythm. As the first sent Saint spinning off balance to dodge, the third lowered his shoulder and plowed into her. The two careened across the tiled floor and into the back wall, knocking equipment to the floor. Without hesitating, Saint twisted her body and wrapped her thighs around the High Wraith's head. Pushing off the wall, she flipped him onto his back. With her legs still firmly around his neck, she twisted hard until she heard a crack. Watching his eyes flutter and roll back, she cautiously stood up. He wasn't dead, but he wouldn't be rejoining the fight any time soon. Pointing at the remaining two High Wraiths, she lifted her hand and tauntingly waved them in.

Reaching into their coats, they pulled their scythes and snapped them open. Saint twisted her head to the right and popped her neck. Smiling, she charged back into the fray. As the first brought his scythe over and down, Saint avoided the attack and stomped the edge of the weapon to the ground with her heavy booted foot. Catching the second High Wraith's scythe in her hand, she yanked him closer and threw a punch directly into the bridge of his nose. Blood instantly gushed from the break, spilling down over his lips. The first leaned in and delivered a vicious headbutt. Saint stumbled back, stunned, and with stars in her eyes, let go of the weapon. Keeping the point on the ground, the High Wraith used the weapon as a pole and vaulted into Saint. His feet hit her squarely in the chest, knocking her to the ground. Rolling forward, he landed on top of her, pinning her arms beneath his legs.

Pressing his scythe into her throat, he stared at her with no emotion whatsoever. "You will stop this," he commanded.

Saint gasped for breath as he ground the scythe harder into her throat. She watched the second High Wraith cross the room quickly and begin to tend to the third. Looking back up at the first, she knew she had been beaten. She tried to speak, but couldn't gather enough air to form the words. A nod would have to suffice.

The first High Wraith held his position a moment longer. "If you try to escape again, I will kill you."

Saint stared into his eyes. He wasn't lying. She nodded again.

Standing up, the High Wraith snapped his scythe closed and returned it to his jacket. Taking a step back, he lowered his hand to Saint, palm open. After a moment of hesitation, Saint accepted his hand. Lifting her from the floor, the two weary combatants sized each other up. "You fought well."

"Not well enough," she said with a smirk. She felt the presence of the second High Wraith behind her. "You two are still standing."

"You do understand, you had no chance of defeating three High Wraiths," the second said from behind her.

Saint felt a sharp pinch in her lower back. Jumping away from the second High Wraith, she spun to see a spent syringe in his hand. Odd warmth began to spread through her flesh. "What did you…?" Reaching out, Saint grabbed the side of the table to steady herself. Her knees buckled, dropping to the floor in a heap.

"Was that really necessary?" the first High Wraith asked.

The second High Wraith wiped some of the blood away from his mouth and nose. "Did you see what that bitch did to me? Yeah, it was necessary."

The first shook his head. "What a waste. She

took on three of us and nearly won." He looked down at Saint. "We need her out there, not down here in some damn lab."

"Not our decision," the second reminded him quickly. "If the council wants her here, then that's all we need to know." He lifted his jacket and tried to wipe away more of the blood. "She does pack one helluva wallop though."

Taking a deep breath, he looked at Saint a moment longer before turning back to his companion. "Strap her to the table and pick him up," he said, pointing to the third High Wraith. "Let's get out of here."

***

Whipping his coat around in a flourish, Quinn hugged the wall as he moved. Coming around a corner, he flattened himself and stopped. He could see the sun beginning to rise in the east through one of the few windows in the mansion not completely boarded up. He had spent most of the night searching the mansion and so far, had been able to avoid detection. This place was old and rotting. The decaying floorboards creaked if he looked at them wrong. It had taken all of his skill to remain unnoticed.

The vampires he had been tracking had disappeared into the lower levels of the house some time ago. As far as Quinn could tell, there was only one entrance. Using it would surely leave him vulnerable to attack, as it was no doubt, guarded. He had observed several more groups of vampires use that same entrance. There must be a stronghold there. He had to get access. There had to be another way in, he just had to find it.

Taking a few more steps, he noticed the unmistakable glow of candlelight flickering against the wall. Moving cautiously and carefully, he placed his hand on the pommel of his scythe. Stopping at the edge of the wall, he craned his neck and peered around the edge. The floor ahead had given way, leaving a gaping hole lined with jagged splinters of wood and metal. Glancing down, he could see several vampires, including his original quarry, milling about. One was leaning back in a chair and had fallen asleep, while the others were playing cards. A low muttering caught his attention. Scanning across the room, Quinn spotted a naked woman in a cage near the edge. She was curled into the fetal position and visibly shaking. Another cage sat in the opposite corner, although it was empty. Apparently, it had held the main course. He returned his gaze to the woman; she was obviously intended for dessert. Two of the vampires started toward her cage.

Moving slightly closer to the edge of the hole, Quinn heard a board squeak under his foot. Holding his breath, he dropped down and flattened himself to the floor. He strained his ears for a moment to listen. The vampires hadn't detected him, hadn't even paused. They were probably used to this house's voice, Quinn reassured himself, and they had dulled their senses to it. Inching noiselessly forward, he grasped onto the edge and peered inside. He quickly counted fifteen to twenty

116

vampires in the room, too many for a single Wraith to tackle. A Wraith was an even match for a single vampire, but in this case, he was desperately outnumbered.

He returned his attention to the woman. The two vampires were teasing her and rattling the cage. Pushing herself into the furthest corner, she brought her knees up and buried her face. Her long blond hair spilled over her trembling flesh. Snapping open the door, the first vampire—a ghoulish specimen dressed head to toe in black leather with a tall, purple mohawk—stepped inside. Unbuckling his belt, he unsnapped the first button on his leather pants. Quinn gritted his teeth as he watched. Laughing to his companion, Mohawk grabbed the girl and shook her like a rag doll. As she started to scream, he reached into his coat pocket and retrieved a blood red handkerchief and stuffed it deep into her mouth. Satisfied, he spun her naked body in his arms and bent her over. Pulling out his erect penis with his free hand, he forcefully spread her legs and penetrated her. Quinn cringed as the second vampire headed into the cage with what he was sure was similar motives.

Rolling onto his back, he struggled to think of a way to get her out of there without killing both of them. Looking up, he caught a glimpse of a shadow moving along the roof in the darkness above him. Before he had a chance to pull his scythe, the shadow leapt toward him with his golden eyes blazing. The force of the vampire landing on top of him sent them both crashing through the already corroded floor. The two smashed through the

117

middle of the table the vampires had been playing at, sending cards, money, and creatures careening in every direction. Quinn landed flat on his back, while the vampire landed perfectly on the balls of his feet.

Gasping for air, Quinn rolled onto his side and drew his scythe. As he snapped it open, he forcefully took command of his body. Sucking down a painful breath, he lurched up into a standing position just as the vampire took a swipe at him. Whipping his scythe up with a flourish, he focused his mind. There was no choice now. He had to fight. Avoiding another attack by the vampire who had brought him down, Quinn retaliated. Rushing ahead, he snapped his scythe between the vampire's legs and twisted, sending the creature spilling to the floor. Before the vampire had a chance to move, Quinn stamped his foot onto its throat and brought his scythe down firmly into the creature's chest. As blue flame shot up from the wound, the Master Wraith pulled his weapon free and addressed the ones remaining.

Glancing across the room, he saw Mohawk and his companion pulling up their pants as they exited the cage. Fifteen vampires stood between him and the woman. There was only one option open to him: charge. With a flourish, he brought his weapon up and tapped the button, again activating the curved blade at the tip. Charging forward, he ran directly through the center of the vampires, his scythe creating a razor sharp barrier. Snapping it laterally across his body, he easily excised one of the vampire's arms. Twisting his head around, he

118

spotted Mohawk closing in. A little retribution is in order, he told himself.

As Quinn moved to intercept, another vampire stepped directly in his path. Whipping his scythe around his body, he lowered it and turned the blade up. Catching the creature in the groin, Quinn pulled the blade up and free from the vampire's chest. As the creature clasped its hands around its crotch, it fell to the floor in a blue blaze. Knocking a third aside with the butt of his weapon, the Wraith found himself face to face with Mohawk.

Diving forward, Quinn hit the purple-haired vampire in the forehead with the side of his scythe. As Mohawk stumbled back, Quinn spun his scythe around his back, dropped down to one knee, and brought the blade cleanly though Mohawk's knee. The punk vampire crumbled to the ground with a shriek as blood sprayed from the ad hoc amputation. Rolling forward onto his feet, Quinn pressed his foot against Mohawk's face and brought the point of his blade down into the punk's brain. Ripping it free, he lopped off the top of Mohawk's head. As he screamed and convulsed on the floor, Quinn turned back to the other vampires.

He didn't have time for this. Cutting down the closest attacker, Quinn flipped his scythe closed and charged forward. Leaping off the ground in a move that could only be described as superhuman, he flipped once in the air and landed in a dead run toward the woman's cage. Tearing open the metal door, he reached in and pulled the frightened woman out. As he lifted her into his arms, he felt the sharp sting of claws shredding down his back.

With a grunt, he threw his head back and connected with the vampire's chin. As the monster grunted and fell back, Quinn charged for the door. Easily kicking it open, he skittered into the hallway and slammed it shut. Pressing his back against the door and propping a foot against the opposite wall, he felt a hard thud. It wouldn't take them long to get through.

Quinn looked down at the naked woman in his arms. "Woman" was an overestimate. She was little more than a child of fifteen or sixteen. Lacerations covered much of her body. Her blue eyes were blackened and her lips swollen. She had been down here for a while. There was no way both would make it out. He had to buy her some time. Setting her down on her feet, he quickly pulled off his tattered coat and handed it to her. Pressing his back to the door again, he watched her gratefully pull it on.

Quinn pointed up the stars. "Run!"

The girl shook her head. She didn't want to leave him.

"I don't have time to argue," he said, turning her toward the stairs. "Run!"

"Merci," she said sweetly, "merci." Turning away from Quinn, she ran up the stairs and threw open the door. Cautiously peering out, she charged out of the doorway and into the mansion.

Quinn took a breath and prayed that she would make it to the door just as two hands erupted from the door and wrapped around his throat. Yanking hard, they pulled the Wraith through the wooden door and back into the room. Slamming him on the floor, three vampires piled on him and held him down. Quinn waited. He knew for sure they would gang up and tear him to pieces. To his surprise, the vampires surrounding him took a step back.

Quinn watched as a figure clad in a midnight black robe entered the circle and strode confidently toward him. The figure stepped into a shaft of light, exposing his rusted facemask. Dropping down next to the Wraith, he placed his gloved hand on Quinn's forehead. "You fought well," Bane commended, "but your weakness was the woman."

"Nice mask," Quinn spat.

Bane snapped his fingers. Two vampires walked into the room with the girl in tow. Stripping off her borrowed coat, they displayed her in front of Quinn. He looked at her in apology. The two vampires savagely bit into her throat. The woman screamed, but it was lost in a weakening gurgle in her throat as her body became limp. They then dropped the girl's dead body to the floor and turned to face their master, her blood still fresh on their lips.

"You bastard," Quinn breathed.

"If you hadn't stopped for her, you both might've lived." Bane turned and started to walk away. "Bring the Wraith. I am in need of his services," he instructed over his shoulder.

***

Her jaw throbbed as she lifted herself from the cold, hard floor. Pushing herself up onto her knees, she saw a small smear of blood on the tiled floor.

Wiping the side of her hand across her lip, she pulled away more. Brigitte glanced up at the steel table she had previously been strapped to. Sometime during her blackout, the guards must have removed the restraints and she had fallen off. She quickly turned her head toward the door, expecting to see the two vampire guards looming there, but instead, found nothing. Cocking her head slightly, she rubbed her wrists and slowly stood.

She was alone for the first time since Stephanov was slain. Her mind wandered back to that night. She shuddered at the memory of watching his body being shredded by the explosion—the same one that claimed her leg. The thought of seeing his flesh, bones, and organs haplessly scattered about the ground sickened her. This was a man she respected, one she loved—and he had been stolen from her. Anger began to skitter up her spine toward her brain, threatening to explode into pure, raw rage. As she propped herself against the table, she could hear her knuckles popping in protest as she squeezed the edge. A single image erupted into her brain: Bane's rusted mask. Her lips curled back into a sneer, "Ba–"

Shooting pain seared through her vocal chords, stopping her in midsyllable. As if being choked by some unseen hand, she fell forward onto the table. Her body flopped and convulsed like a fish that had been ripped from the water. Snapping forward involuntarily, her forehead smacked hard against the steel table. Silver and gold spots exploded in front of her eyes. Stumbling back, her rage began to subside as it was replaced with fear. Lifting her

122

hands to her throat, she took a deep, pain-filled breath. Her windpipe was bruised. She could feel five painful spots on her neck as if fingertips had been digging into it.

Falling to the floor, she pushed herself against the tiled wall and took another breath. Moving her hands up her face, she ran her fingertips lightly over her forehead. She could feel a lump forming. It was a good sign that at least she hadn't fractured the bone and caused a concussion. Her heart shook and jumped behind her rib cage as adrenaline coursed through her veins. She remembered her confrontation with Bane just before her blackout. He had poured something down her throat. It tasted somewhat like blood and had a similar viscosity, but it wasn't exactly human, or vampire, for that matter. She remembered it burning like acid as she was forced to swallow. He had done something to her, changed her—morphed her into something. She could still taste the fluid in the back of her throat. Swallowing hard, she tried to get past it.

She closed her eyes for a moment to allow her mind to relax. Her mental projection flickered briefly, but remained intact. It was a chore to keep the illusion intact, more so for some vampires like Brigitte. The virus that created vampires amplified the natural gifts of humans, especially those directly dealing with extra sensory perception and telekinesis. But if the subject didn't have the tools to begin with, there was only so much the virus could do. Keeping up her illusion was mentally taxing, yet she would not let it fall. The mere sight of a "natural" vampire sickened her. Her kind should be perfect, beautiful, powerful, and proud—not twisted, grotesque corpses.

She felt a twinge of sensation on her forearm. Brushing her hand over the area, she paid no more attention to it. Pushing the hair from her face, she felt something creeping up her arm again. Opening her eyes, she looked down to find a large, black spider perched just above her hand. Knowing that there was nothing the spider could do to hurt her, even if it was venomous, she shook her hand and knocked the arachnid to the floor. Leaning over on her elbow, she cocked her fingers and flicked the bug across the room. It made a satisfying crunch as it impacted the opposite wall and died. At least it was now having a worse day than she was.

She had to get out of here, yet she had no idea where "here" was. An idea occurred to her: Stephanov had an elite group of Wraith hunters who were not with him during the assassination. If she could contact them, it would be an easy task to set them lose on Bane. These creatures had trained their entire existence to hunt the hunters, so a pack of vampires should be no problem. Theoretically, she reminded herself.

She was stopped in mid-thought by something crawling on her back. Shaking her head, she reached over her shoulder and grabbed the offending sensation. Bringing it back around in front of her, she opened her hand to find another big, black spider. Lifting it, she prepared to fling it across the room with its friend. As her eyes focused on the far side of the room, she stopped. The dead spider was gone. Lowering her hand, she looked at the bug. It was very similar to the one that had been on her arm. It was more than similar, she noticed, it was identical. Tossing the creature away, she felt her temples throbbing. Watching the spider on the floor, she felt something on her chest. Glancing down, she saw another identical black spider clinging to the flesh just above the cut of her dress. Knocking the arachnid away with the back of her hand, she pulled herself away from the wall.

Turning, she saw at least fifteen spiders clinging to the wall just above where she had been. The hair on the back of her neck stood up as she felt the now familiar sensation on her scalp. Tossing her hair forward, she yanked another spider from the back of her head and smashed it against the wall with her open palm. Looking down, she saw hundreds of the beasts skittering toward her feet in one mighty black wave. Stumbling back, her hands hit against the silver table. Instantly, she could feel several spiders latching onto them. Spinning abruptly, she tossed the bugs away, only to find dozens more on the tabletop. As the first of the spiders began to crawl up her legs, Brigitte tried vainly to knock them away, but there were too many. For every one she killed, there were ten more that took its place.

Stifling a scream in her sore throat, she charged toward the door. The crunching under her feet sickened her. Latching her hand onto the doorknob, she twisted hard, only to find it locked. Twisting her body, she reared back and threw her shoulder into the door with all of her strength. It didn't even budge. She felt the spiders moving up her back toward her neck. Grunting, she hit the door again, and then again. The spiders were all over her, biting, crawling, and spinning their webs. Her skin crawled with revulsion. Stepping back, she crossed her arms over her face and threw her entire body at the door. She exploded through amidst a rain of debris.

She hit the stone floor hard, her momentum still carrying her forward. As she skidded, she suddenly felt weightless. Without a moment's hesitation, her hands shot out in an instinctual act of self-preservation. Grabbing onto the edge, she swung her feet over and hit the wall hard. Holding tightly, she tried to dig her fingers into the edge and pull herself up. Looking back, she stared into the pitch black maw of a circular pit located just a few feet beyond the door. At least twenty feet in diameter, the pit was immense. Breathing a sigh of relief, she propped her elbow up on the lip and started to pull herself out. Glancing back into the room, she could find no trace of the spiders. Her temples began to throb again. Feeling lightheaded, she hurriedly tried to lift herself out before she blacked out. Pushing up with her hands, she kicked her leg easily up onto the edge. Twisting her body over, she rested on the edge of the pit, her arm dangling over. She strained to find a moment of clarity. But it was fleeting as she felt something brush against her hand.

"More damned spiders," she groaned.

Before she could pull it away, something clamped down hard around her wrist and yanked her free of her perch. With a gasp, Brigitte was back over the side of the pit. Grasping onto the edge with her opposite hand, she struggled against the force pulling her in. Looking down, her eyes widened in horror. A decaying, skeletal hand had emerged from the darkness of the pit and was wrapped around her arm. Several more hands suddenly appeared and began clawing at her legs. As they pulled her further into the darkness, Brigitte strained her fingers trying to hold on. As the clawed fingers bit and tore into her flesh, she grunted in pain. Two more hands latched onto her ankles and yanked her body harder. Screaming through the pain in her throat, she fought against the hands. More and more emerged from the inky blackness and clamped onto her. She felt her fingers begin to slip. Clawing hard, her grip loosened. With a scream, her fingers slipped off the edge and she tumbled into the darkness.

Snapping her head up with a start, she flailed her arms wildly. Reaching out for anything, her hand hit against the metal table. With a start, she stopped. Opening her eyes wide, she glanced around the room in confusion. She was back in the room she started in. Glancing across the room, she found the door completely intact and no trace of the spiders could be seen. Lifting her hand to her forehead, she searched for the bump she had received when hitting her head. Her fingertips ran through a warm, sticky patch. Pulling her fingers away, she saw several daubs of blood on the tips. As her eyes rolled back in her head, she fell back to the floor and lost consciousness.

CHAPTER EIGHT

Saint opened her eyes slowly. Trying to sit up, a rush of pain hit her squarely in the front lobe of her brain. Falling back, she took a deep breath to center herself. Licking her dry lips, she glanced up. The fluorescent lights in the ceiling hurt her eyes. Blinking rapidly, she tried to adjust to the light. Lifting her hand, she ran it gently over her forehead. Her fingertips caught the edge of adhesive tape and stopped. Moving slowly left, she felt a gauze pad held firmly in place by the tape. She could feel a solid area on the gauze signaling the presence of dried blood. Looking down, she noticed for the first time she was completely nude. A thin sheet covering her from her chest to her thighs was barely covering her body. Several electrodes were attached to her temples and her chest. A tube ran from a long needle in the back of her hand up to a clear plastic package of fluid. Feeling weak and groggy, she realized there was more in the fluid than just saline and pulled the needle from her hand.

Wrapping her hand across her chest to keep the sheet in place, she slowly sat up. Again, the dull throb of pain hit her. Closing her eyes and holding her breath, she waited for the pain to subside. Exhaling slowly, she opened her eyes and glanced around the medical bay. Everything from her scuffle earlier with the High Wraiths had been put to rights, making her wonder exactly how long she had been unconscious. Swinging her legs over the edge of the table, the constant beep of the heart monitor filled her ears. She glanced around the room. There were no windows and she could see no signs of surveillance equipment, but she knew it was there. She had to get free of this place. Pushing off the table, her soft flesh squeaked against the side. As she hit the floor, her mind was swimming from the drugs. She could feel her balance wavering, threatening to topple her at any moment.

Holding steady, she spotted a pile of clothes in the corner. Saint walked carefully across the floor, making sure to use her hands to steady herself. Reaching down, she picked up the first article of clothing and frowned. It was her leather pants, and they were shredded. They had cut her clothes off of her. Glancing down at the floor, she spotted her chunky, black boots. At least they're okay, she thought. Turning, she spotted a folded pair of nurse's scrubs sitting on a countertop. Snatching up the light green clothes, she set the small sheet aside and pulled on the pants. Tying the drawstring waist tightly, she pulled on the v-neck top. It was huge on her slim frame, hanging almost halfway down her thighs. Dropping down into a nearby chair, she grabbed her boots and pulled them on. Standing up, she felt like she was drowning in the outfit, but it would have to do.

Moving back to the door, she peered out through the long, rectangular window that ran up the side of it. Through the metal crosshatching embedded in it, she could see the hall was empty. Slowly wrapping her hand around the handle, she gently twisted the doorknob. As the bolt disengaged, she started to pull the heavy door open.

Peering through the crack, she scanned the hallway again. Satisfied that it was empty, she stepped into the hall and turned toward the elevator. Moving quickly and quietly, she stopped just short of the doors. Her mind snapped back to the image of the keypad just inside. She hadn't seen what the code had been. Knowing there was no way to activate the elevator without it, her mind whirred, trying to find another option.

Reaching out, she pulled open the heavy doors and stepped inside. Glancing around the rickety elevator, her eyes settled on the brushed aluminum surface of the keypad. Saint clasped her hands around it and tried to yank it off the wall. Pulling again, her fingers slipped off as the panel refused to budge. With a grunt, she slid her now broken thumbnail into her mouth. Feeling the broken ridge with her tongue, she pulled her hand free and tried to shake away the tingling sensation of pain. Turning back into the elevator, she glanced up at the ceiling. It looked like a solid sheet of metal. Cocking her head slightly, she noticed a thin seam around the single light in the center. Rising onto her toes, she pushed on the light with her fingertips. Her heart thumped in her chest as she felt it budge.

Reaching over, she clasped onto the metal grating that surrounded the elevator and lifted herself toward the ceiling. Stretching out, she flattened her palm and slapped her hand hard up against the panel. With a groan, it flipped up and open as bits of paint broke away and flittered toward the floor. Reaching back, Saint grasped the edge and pulled herself easily through the small service hatch. Dropping the hatch back into place, she glanced up the elevator shaft. Nearly dark except for the regular intervals of red lights that lined the walls, the shaft seemed to be endless. No trace of the top could be seen through the darkness that hung like a haze above her.

To her left, she could see a slim ladder that looked to lead up to the top. Clasping onto the cool, metal rungs, Saint pulled herself onto the ladder. Pacing herself, she started slowly up, her mind still groggy. The sound of her hands and feet hitting the metal rungs echoed off the concrete walls into the darkness. Blocking out the dull throb in her temples, she pushed herself forward...but to what?

She had been in training for nearly half her life for no other purpose than to become a Wraith. If she ran now, she would be throwing that all away. Is that what she really wanted? Saint stopped. Slipping her arm into the ladder, she folded her elbow over one of the rungs to rest. She wondered if she should climb back down and just endure the procedures and tests. This certainly wasn't some evil organization with nefarious plans for her particular gifts—this was the Gwyliad Wriaeth, a group with the singular goal of fighting back the darkness for humanity's sake. If they could better their set of "advantages" in this war, wouldn't that better serve the entire Gwyliad Wriaeth? Saint rested her forehead against the cool metal of the ladder and tried to find some clarity. She longed to be out on assignment right now, but that had all been taken away by a quirk of biology. Instead of slinking through the night hunting her prey, she was forced to do her duty inside a laboratory. It wasn't fair, she told herself, but it was her destiny.

Climbing back down the ladder, she dropped on top of the elevator. Kneeling down, she pulled open the service hatch. Dropping her legs over the edge, she placed her hands on the edge and slipped inside. With a heavy heart, she assured herself she was doing the right thing. It wasn't about her anymore—it was about what she could give to her fellow Wraiths. Pulling open the heavy lift doors, she came face-to-face with two High Wraiths waiting for her. She instantly recognized one of them from the scuffle earlier. He had been the one who caught her.

She looked up into their stoic faces. "Why didn't you follow me into the elevator?"

"The decision was yours," the High Wraith said softly and honestly. "We knew you would make the correct choice."

"And if I didn't?"

The Wraith smiled slyly. "We had close to twenty Wraiths waiting at the top of the elevator for you."

Saint shook her head. "Nice."

Reaching out, the High Wraith placed his hand on the young woman's shoulder. "We thought so."

Turning, the two High Wraiths led Saint back to her room. Glancing back over her shoulder, Saint thought of her freedom one last time. Resigning herself, she turned away from the elevator. She was doing this for the good of the Wraith, she half-heartedly reminded herself.

***

Falling to his knees, he wrapped his arm across his stomach, fighting the urge to vomit. As he lifted his head toward the darkened sky, he forced a breath down into his burning lungs. Gritting his teeth, he fought. He wanted to fall to the ground, to lay his arms down, but he couldn't. It wouldn't allow him. He had a task to complete. It burned in his mind like a fire, raging across his memories and emotions. It compelled him from his knees and sent him surging once again toward his target. Balling his fists, his body lurched forward. Working against each step, he looked as if some unseen tether were pulling him.

His face and body were battered and bruised. Several of his ribs and fingers were broken and large lacerations covered his face and continued down over his throat. He had been through worse, but he couldn't remember when. The pain was all-consuming. Vivid flashes of his capture and torture ran rampant through his brain. He could see their claws, their fangs, ripping, tearing, and cutting at his flesh. Down in that place, he had lost all sense of time. Weeks could have passed in there, or it could have been merely hours. His memories were not to be trusted anymore. They had taken all he held dear and twisted it inside his mind. His senses, his gifts, were working against him now. He was merely a passenger in his own body, no more able to control his limbs than those of another person. He hated them for it. He hated himself.

Anger welled up from the base of his skull, but

it was not directed at those who had held and tortured him, it was all for his target. Confusion underpinned the wave of anger. They were not his enemy…how could he hate them so? As his body lurched forward, he pressed the meaty part of his palms against his swollen and bruised eyes. He gasped once under his breath. His emotions were starting to break down. Rage, anger, confusion, fear, and pain all seemed to blend into a single muddy concoction that washed over his body and threatened to pull him asunder. In his mind, he tumbled endlessly into the abyss, each moment, the light at the top growing dimmer. He was losing his grasp.

Coming up over a small rise, he could see the lights of the town glowing. He was almost there and then he could rest. In some dim corner of his mind, he felt a tinge of relief. Release was nearing.

Stumbling down the hill, he nearly lost his footing near the bottom. Quickly regaining his balance, he lifted his head and glanced into the distance at his target. He moved forward along the quiet streets amid the sleeping homes and empty businesses. Peering through his eyes as if watching a movie, he screamed, but couldn't force any sound from his throat. If he could alert them—anyone—they could stop him. Silence. Only the sound of the nearby coast filled his ears. Something deep in his mind compelled him to wrap his coat tightly around his chest, hiding his dark secret. Crossing his arms, he felt the edge of the package he had been tasked with delivering. If only he could reach down and remove it…his hands shook as he fought against his own muscles.

Glancing up, he felt a wave of dread hit his body like a hammer. Reaching out, he pulled open the front gates as he had done a thousand times before, and stepped inside the courtyard. It was quiet here. He knew there would be guards, but his entrance had been timed to catch them during shift change. Closing his eyes, he fought through the haze in his mind to find some focus. He could feel his body moving toward the front entrance. Each muscle contraction, each step, he was almost there. As he clenched his jaw, anger hit him again. They were responsible and they would be made to pay. They were not his words and yet, they burned like acid in his chest. He felt every horrible syllable, each individual letter as it swirled in his thoughts. They had become his, or rather, they had been programmed to become his. He could feel the sheer venom directed against this place and those it contained. He held them responsible and retribution was at hand.

Turning to his left, he spotted a guard coming around the side of the building. If he could call out, make a sound; signal him in anyway…he turned away. Watching his hand reach out, it pushed the double doors open. Warmth spilled from the well-lit interior over his body. It was calm here, peaceful. This place was a sanctuary. Every bone, every muscle, every sinew of his body longed to collapse to the floor, but he could not. His task was at hand.

"Master Quinn?"

Quinn turned slowly to see an approaching High Wraith. He recognized this man, and had served with him in battle on numerous occasions. He was a cunning warrior, and a good friend—yet Quinn's blood ran cold at the sight of him. The long coat, the gleaming scythe at his side, the deep red of the fabric on his vest, how he hated them.

Clenching his teeth, he closed his eyes and fought against the rage not his own. As a lone tear fell down his cheek, he achieved a moment of clarity. Looking apologetically up at his friend, he opened his tattered black coat wide. Only one thought rolled off Quinn's tongue:

"Kill me."

The High Wraith's eyes widened as he skidded to a stop. There, strapped to Quinn's torso, were enough explosives to put a dent in the Earth. A spider's web of red, black, and blue wire interconnected the numerous bricks of C4. Amidst the sea of plastic explosives sat the trigger. Situated directly in the middle of Quinn's chest, it was designed in a small, plastic, black box. Three red LED lights adorned the front and blinked at regular intervals. A sleek, silver toggle switch sat directly below them.

Without another moment's hesitation, he drew his scythe and charged toward Quinn. Activating the weapon, he started his swing…

But Quinn was faster.

With Bane's voice screaming in his head, Quinn pressed his thumb against the toggle, closed his eyes and activated it. A high-pitched whine filled the air as the trigger charged up. Instantly, an electrical pulse was sent along the wires toward the blocks of explosives. As the first charge hit, the

Wraith Academy was turned from a sanctuary into a hellish blaze. Within milliseconds, the other bricks of C4 detonated, killing Quinn and the High Wraith instantly. As the blast and accompanying fireball ripped through the main building, the electricity flickered once and died as load-bearing walls were toppled. The force of the explosion leveled the main entrance and brought the ceiling down around them. Large sections of the floor were blown in, revealing the hidden structure beneath. Screams and the blaring sound of fire alarms tore through the once calm night.

It was done, and he could rest now. May all those he killed tonight forgive him for his weakness.

***

Saint sat up amidst the tubes and wires attached to her. Moments earlier, the attending physician and a group of nurses had exited the room after a grueling forty-five minute exam. As the lights flickered and died above her, she sat quietly in the darkness of the medical bay, her arms still sore from the copious amounts of blood that had been drawn. A low rumble filled her ears. Around her, she could feel the walls and ceiling shaking. Without making a move to find shelter, she placed her hand on her chest. Taking a long, slow breath, she felt a deep sadness cut through her. As if her heart had been pulled from her chest while still beating, she felt a gaping hole within.

She sensed it somewhere deep inside her:

137

Master Quinn was dead.

She closed her eyes and bowed her head. Falling back to the table, she felt a single tear run down her cheek. Rolling onto her side, she slid off the metal table onto the balls of her feet. Placing her palms flat on the cool surface, she drew a deep breath and choked back her tears. Gritting her teeth, she felt her face flush with anger. Balling her fists, she snapped her arms high over her head and brought them down full force toward the center of the table. The solid metal surface folded under the force of the blow. Stumbling back from the destruction, Saint fell to the floor. She pushed herself back to the wall and pulled her knees tightly to her chest.

PART THREE

One Will...

It will not be easy.

Everything you held dear is gone, yet you can become stronger from the experience or resign your fate.

To give completely to the path demands total devotion and complete sacrifice. Your will must not be bent to that of destiny and the fates. You must take what has been placed before you and make it your own.

It will not be easy.

But you must choose to walk the path.

It is yours alone.

CHAPTER NINE

A dark form hovered on a hill overlooking the Wraith Academy, its dark cloak billowing in the wind. Unmoving, he stared down into the destruction he had wrought. Crossing his arms, Bane enjoyed a moment of pure satisfaction watching the smoke waft out of the crater he had created. The red flames of the fire licked high into the sky above the wreckage, creating a red glow that could be seen for miles. The meager town's emergency vehicles gathered around the front of the building, trying helplessly to contain the fire and help the survivors of the tragedy. Their red and blue lights flashed and reflected off the walls of the nearby buildings and homes. It was perfect. It was chaos. It was beyond his wildest dreams.

Turning reluctantly away from the scene, his golden eyes surveyed the creatures standing before him. Each bore a twisting, winding, black tribal tattoo on their face—his mark. They stood patiently, waiting for his command, their eyes fixed on him. There were easily two hundred men and women here tonight, each thirsty for battle and the viscous red substance that sustained them. He was pleased. His various campaigns across Europe had all led to this moment. He had been conducting battle drills against the other vampire lords for no other purpose than to weed out the weak amongst his ranks. As he looked over his army now, all he could see was power. And he was pleased.

"Wipe them out," he boomed to his army, "all of them!"

As his army charged down into the town, Bane turned to his silent companion, his golden eyes burning with pleasure. Tossing back his black cloak, he lifted his arms and held them straight out. Stepping out of the darkness, she lifted two long, curved blades and began to strap them to her master's arms. As she finished tightening down the leather straps that held the weapons in place, she bowed her head. Bane admired the blades for a moment as they gleamed in the moonlight. Thrusting his arms down, the blades automatically snapped back on a hinge and lay vertically against his arms.

Lifting one arm, he reached out and took his companion's hand. "Are you ready?"

Stepping forward, she pulled the hood back on her midnight black robe allowing her wavy, chocolate hair to fall forward. "I am, my Lord." A thin, black, swirling tribal tattoo ran down the side of her face.

"Very good," Bane cackled, "Brigitte."

***

A flash of light glinted off the surface of the table. Lifting her head slowly, she glanced around the room, almost unsure that she had even seen it. Dropping her head back against the wall, she tried to wipe the tears from her face with the heel of her hand. As she took a deep breath to try and calm her nerves, she spotted the light again. It looked to her like the beam of a flashlight being shone through the vertical window in the door.

Naked, cold, and in pain, she didn't want to be found, at least not yet. She cursed under her breath. She would have been content to stay down here in the darkness. There was no sound to distract her, no hum of electricity. No steady throb of the air-conditioning system. It was utterly quiet. She could hear her own heart beating and the long, slow breaths as her lungs processed the oxygen in the air. She could revel in her own inner darkness without distraction or reprieve. She hadn't realized it until now, but the bond she and Master Quinn had developed had progressed far beyond that of teacher and apprentice. Only now, when it was gone, did she understand. Anger flashed behind her eyes for a moment, but quickly dissolved in the inky darkness. She would have retribution, but right now, she needed to grieve more than anything else.

The door of the medical bay slowly opened, the hinges grinding loudly in the silence. Two beams of bright, white light sliced through the darkness until they landed on her. Looking up, Saint squinted her eyes and held her hand in front of her face to block the light. "Would you get those damn things off me?"

The lights quickly lowered. She could make out three figures entering the room. The first was obviously a High Wraith. She noticed the light glinting off his red vest. The two others were a bit harder to make out, as they seemed to be hiding behind the High Wraith. The scent of fear was heavy on those two. They were not Wraiths. No one trained by the Academy would be that afraid of the dark. Saint guessed they were either medical or

142

technical personnel who were trapped here when the power went out.

Moving steadily into the bay, the High Wraith stopped by Saint and dropped down next to her. "Are you okay?" He reached for her, but stopped, unsure of what he should do. His short-cropped hair was a mess of blood and dust as a jagged cut sliced from within his hairline and spilled down onto his forehead. A solid streak of blood ran from the cut down the side of his face and over his eye. Dirt and grime were caked on his strong features. Saint thought he resembled the pictures of underground coal miners she had seen in textbooks. His once strong blue eyes were now battered and tired. This man, who was among the Wraith's inner circle and had apparently been charged with keeping watch over her, looked defeated.

Saint looked up into the High Wraith's face. She didn't recognize him, but that wasn't too surprising. There were many High Wraiths in the council's employ. "I'm fine." She took a slow breath. "What the hell is going on?"

The Wraith shook his head. "We have no idea. We've been completely cut off from the surface levels."

"Emergency power?" Saint queried.

"Nothing," the High Wraith replied. "Our options are running a little low right now. We've been focusing on searching for survivors."

"Survivors?" Saint asked in shock. "How bad is it out there?"

The High Wraith made no attempt to hide his emotions. "Very." Setting his rectangular flashlight on the ground, he flipped the switch to activate a small fluorescent light built into the side. As the small light flickered to life, the room was filled with an eerie blue light. "Something serious must have gone down on top," he said slowly, "major portions of the underground complex have collapsed in and others seem to be on the verge of following suit. The Academy compound was built to be self-contained with four massive clean water tanks just below the second level. One of those seems to have ruptured, flooding the third level entirely."

"Jesus," Saint breathed.

"That's not the best part," the High Wraith continued. "Both elevator shafts leading to the surface have been compromised."

"Leaving us with what?"

The High Wraith closed his eyes for a moment. "Little to nothing."

Saint nodded. "What's the plan?"

The High Wraith dropped his gaze.

"That good, huh?" Saint quickly resolved herself.

This was a crisis. They needed more than a scared little girl to take care of. They needed someone to rely on. If it wasn't going to be the High Wraith, then it would be her. Grabbing the flashlight off the floor, she stood and set it on the edge of the smashed examination table, revealing to the others for the first time that she was completely naked. Glancing back at the men over her shoulder, she watched them all quickly snap their stares away from her flesh. Shaking her head, she walked around the table toward where they had deposited her clothes. Grabbing the green scrubs she had stolen earlier from the floor, she pulled them over her thin frame and started to lace up her boots.

Turning, she placed her hands flat on the table and addressed the three men before her. "We need to get our asses out of here."

"We need to try and locate more survivors," one of the lab techs chimed in for the first time.

"I agree," Saint said quickly. "If we encounter any survivors, we won't abandon them, but we can't waste our time scouring the entire facility. Our first priority must be getting to the surface. It's imperative that we find out what happened. Once there, we can alert them that there are people down here who need immediate medical attention." She looked at the three men. "What are your names?"

The High Wraith stood and dusted himself off, trying to retain at least some of his dignity. All at once, he looked both relived and worried that Saint had taken charge. "I'm Xavier. Xav," he added with a shrug.

"Carl," the first med tech said. He was wearing almost identical green scrubs over his bulky body. His head was bald, except for a tightly cropped patch of hair that ran from his temples around the back of his head. A pack of cigarettes was rolled in the sleeve of his shirt. He looked to be in his late thirties, possibly early forties. He was overweight, but not noticeably so. He wore it well.

Saint nodded. Turning to the last man, she smiled. "And you?"

The young man, who appeared to be about her

age, averted his gaze. "I'm Mark," his voice quivered. He was handsome, almost too much so to be a med tech. His straight, dark hair hung down over his forehead and just barely covered his left eye. Saint couldn't tell his eye color in the low light, but they captured her. They were powerful, yet subdued. His scrubs were tattered and slightly torn, revealing his muscular frame beneath.

"Very good," she said, realizing she was commenting on Mark more than anything else. "I'm Saint," she added, making no attempt to explain the nickname. "Do we have any more lights?"

"There are a few more in the lab down the hall," Carl replied, "but it's been blocked by debris."

"Any other way in?"

Carl thought for a moment, but shook his head. "I think that's the only way."

Saint started to bite her bottom lip, but quickly stopped. "Okay, then—"

"Unless," Carl interrupted, "the ventilation system is still in good shape."

Saint smiled. "We have a plan." Grabbing the light off the table, she switched it back into flashlight mode and headed toward the door. "Let's get out of here."

CHAPTER TEN

Focusing her preternatural vision into the darkness, Saint led her team further into the complex. Using her flashlight to sweep the floor in front of her, she easily navigated the debris that had fallen from the roof. Entire light banks were dangling dangerously from the ceiling, their stripped wires forming a web that threatened to capture and strangle any who dared to pass. The lingering acrid scent of smoke hung in the air, but no glow of fire could be seen. Running her fingertips along the wall, Saint could detect no residual heat. Easing over a pile of ceiling that had caved in, Saint tried to glance further up the hall.

This place was very similar to the section she had been housed in. The halls were at least ten feet high, sheer white, and curved at the corners. She wondered for a moment if this was how Ripley felt traversing the corridors of the Nostromo as she tried to escape the alien. Even with the debris, these corridors were still much cleaner than those of the future starship envisioned by Ridley Scott in 1979. The crisp white of the walls actually helped her vision in the dark, creating a high contrast surface she could easily see in. She knew now why the walls had been done in this manner.

Glancing back over her shoulder, she quickly took stock of her charges. Each seemed to be handling the situation well, with the notable exception of Xav. How could a High Wraith fold so easily under the stress of the situation? Through training, she had been taught to deal with much worse. Perhaps he had been under the council's control for far too long and had forgotten how to think for himself? Saint chewed her bottom lip gently as she mulled the idea. She didn't buy it. He was hiding something. He should be in charge now. He had the rank and the skill as a High Wraith. To attain his status, one had to be hand selected by the members of the council. High Wraiths were usually decorated war heroes, combat veterans, and powerful warriors. None of these descriptions spoke to her of Xav. Something in the back of her mind gnawed at her. Something wasn't right about this High Wraith, and yet, she couldn't put her finger on it. She would have to be wary.

Carl and Mark, on the other hand, were easier for her to read. They were genuinely scared, as anyone would be. The walked closely together, sharing the second flashlight. Saint sensed they had worked together, perhaps not always on the same crew, but they had spent enough time together to begin forging a friendship. She could tell it was still in its infancy, but something was there. She smiled half-heartedly, reminded of her own relationship with Quinn. These two would watch out for each other down here. That was more than she could say for the sheep in Wraith's clothing who stood between them.

Shaking her head, she focused on the hallway ahead. Sweeping her light up the walls, she spotted a small grate. Holding her light in position, she signaled for Carl to move up. "Take a look."

Carl brought the second light up to bear on the ventilation grate. "That's it."

The grate was situated near the top of the hallway, just below the curve that led into the ceiling. It was roughly rectangular with numerous raised slits on its surface that directed the airflow down into the hall. Although Saint couldn't see clearly, it seemed to be fastened to the wall by several screws. That would be no problem, except she couldn't reach it on her own. At about the nine foot mark on the wall, it was well out of her reach.

"It's so small," Mark said, joining the other two. "None of us can fit through that."

Saint turned and flashed a devious grin at Mark. "I can. I just need a boost." She turned to the Xav. "You should be able to lift me all by yourself."

Xav nodded and stepped forward. Uneasily, he dropped down to one knee and laced his fingertips together. Carefully, Saint placed her foot in his hands. With one easy motion, the High Wraith stood, lifting Saint toward the ventilation grate. Slipping her feet onto his shoulders, she took a moment to steady her balance. Reaching out, she placed her fingertips on the edge of the grate. Like everything else in this place, it was smooth and rounded, giving her no corners to grasp on to. Moving her fingers down the plate, she slid them into two of the raised slits. Wrapping them firmly inside, she yanked once and tore the grate from the wall. As she tossed it to the side, she motioned for Carl to hand her a flashlight. Lifting the bulky light into the vent, she stared deep inside.

"It doesn't seem to be obstructed," Saint breathed, "and I think I'll fit. How far is the lab?"

"It's just on the other side of this wall," he said, tapping the wall with his knuckles. "There should be an intersection not too far in with a vent leading to your right. Follow that in and you should be able to drop down right into the lab. The spare flashlights will be in an emergency cabinet on the north wall."

Saint nodded once. "Lift me up, Xav."

After being pushed up with Xav's enhanced strength, Saint easily pulled herself into the vent. Pushing the flashlight forward, she squeezed into the tight confines of the aluminum. Her shoulders were only centimeters from the walls as she began to crawl forward. Barely able to take a deep breath, the vent groaned and threatened to buckle beneath her. Twisting her head to the right, she peered further ahead of her. Ahead, as predicted by Carl, was an intersection with three branches leading off in different directions. Reaching forward, she placed her hands around the edges of the intersection and pulled herself ahead. Twisting painfully onto her side on the confined space, she glanced up. The intersection was also the destination for a fourth vent leading straight up. She felt a moment of excitement but the orange flickering at the top of the vent quickly quashed it. Through the haze of smoke, she could see the edges of fire licking the ceiling of the vent.

Turning back, she snaked her body around the tight corner and continued on. Sliding the flashlight ahead, she watched it slide along the surface and hit an edge. As the light tumbled to its side, she eagerly moved toward it. Feeling ahead with her fingertips, she felt the familiar edge of a grate built into the bottom of the shaft. Adjusting the light, she set it on the opposite side and pointed it back toward her. Placing her hands flat on the grate, she pushed with all her strength. Amidst the sound of bending metal, the cover broke free. Falling forward, Saint felt the back of her forearm scrape painfully against the exposed metal. Snapping her arm back, she could feel the warmth of blood welling up on the wound.

Ignoring the pain, she grabbed the flashlight and pointed it down into the lab. As she swept the light across the floor, she saw that the lab had been relatively undamaged. Bottles and chairs were knocked down, but that seemed to be the extent of it. Clasping the flashlight handle with her teeth, she pushed her head and torso through the hole. As her waist cleared the edge, she latched on with her hands and gracefully brought her legs twisting over her head until she was hanging from the shaft right-side up. Letting go with one hand, she removed the flashlight from her mouth and dropped easily to the floor.

Swinging the light around, she spotted several cabinets aligned against the north wall of the lab. Moving quickly to the either side, she tossed a few fallen boxes and chairs out of her way. Reaching the first cabinet, she twisted the handle and pulled it open, only to find it completely empty. Slamming the metal door closed in disgust, she moved to the second locker, opened the door and smiled as her luck improved.

***

As the smoke and flames continued to leap into the sky, Bane's vampire army attacked savagely. Tearing through Wraiths and townspeople alike, the vampires rumbled through wreckage and into the Academy. The rescue workers tried to pull more of the injured Wraith from the building, but were mowed down by the advancing onslaught of vampires. The sound of melee—weapons clinging and clanging together—ripped through the constant thrum of the fire. Shrill screams of agonizing pain and death created an unholy cacophony orchestrated by the vampires.

As they moved deeper into the compound, each understood their mission. Seek and destroy. Nothing more. Show no compassion to any living thing within the Academy. Bane wanted nothing more than total obliteration of this main Wraith stronghold. When he and his men completed killing everyone, he would stay and raze the very walls of this place down to the Earth it was constructed on. He would accept nothing less. As he and Brigitte moved behind a line of vampires, their matching black cloaks wafted and billowed around, looking as if they were the very physical manifestation of death surveying its new acquisitions on the battlefield. His metal mask, shadowed by the hood and the night, made his face look dark, almost nonexistent.

Stopping inside the once standing walls of the Academy, the building looked like the dying husk of an animal, its bones jutting high into the night sky. Flames and smoke swirled around the unholy two, exhilarating them. Looking down, Bane stared into the gaping scar the bomb had created in the floor. He could see deep into the hidden underbelly of the Academy. It was a place few new existed, yet its white, sterile walls were familiar to the vampire lord. Returning his gaze up, he watched his army tear into the Academy.

"You will be my general," he said, placing his hand on Brigitte's shoulder. "Take command of my army and see to the plan."

She placed her hand tenderly on his. "Yes, my Lord."

Turning away from Brigitte, Bane flipped his arms forward and snapped his two arm blades into place. Leaping high into the air, he sailed down into the scar.

As Brigitte moved past the hole, she could hear his laughter echoing off the walls. Glancing down, she spotted the charred remains of a Wraith lying amidst the debris and rubble. To her surprise, she saw his lips move. Cocking her head slightly, she stared at the Wraith. He seemed to be mouthing the words, "help me," but no sound was being expelled from his lips. Gritting her fanged teeth, Brigitte lifted her booted foot and brought it down, crushing the Wraith's skull.

***

Carl unrolled his cigarettes from his shirtsleeve. Pulling one of them free of the package, he slid his hand into his pant pocket and retrieved his yellow Bic lighter. Snapping his thumb over the igniter twice, a small, yellow-blue flame jumped up. Lifting it quickly to his cigarette, he took three quick puffs until the end glowed red. Depositing his lighter back into his pocket, he took his first long drag off the cigarette and savored it before exhaling. Glancing across the hallway, he saw Xavier staring intently at him. Twisting his head away, he ignored the Wraith, instead focusing on the darkness that seemed to be encroaching on the white light of their flashlight. It seemed to be drawing closer, but he hoped it was just his imagination. Taking another drag, he blew the blue-gray smoke into the darkness. He spotted Mark sitting on the floor with his legs crossed just in front of one of the larger piles of debris. Mark was sitting quietly trying to pass the time until Saint returned.

Turning away, his eyes landed on the Wraith again. He was still staring at him. "Is my smoking bothering you?"

Xavier shook his head.

"No," Carl laughed, "I guess it's not like you're going to die of cancer."

Xavier's face remained unchanged. He was resting against the wall with his hands clasped behind his back. His unblinking stare seemed to bore straight through Carl's chest and into the wall behind him.

"Can I help you?" Carl asked, slightly agitated.

Xavier said nothing.

"You're starting to freak me out, Chief," Carl admitted nervously. Moving a step to the right, he tried to see if he could break the stare. To his dismay, the Wraith's eyes moved with him.

154

Xavier remained quiet.

"Would you stop fucking staring at me?" Carl shouted.

A wicked smirk grew wide across the Wraith's face. "I'm sorry," he said finally, "was I bothering you?"

"Yes, you creepy motherfucker!" Carl yelled. "Why the hell were you staring at me?"

Xavier shrugged. "Just spaced off I guess."

"What the hell is going on out here?"

All three turned to see Saint's head protruding from the vent shaft. Xavier quickly stepped toward her. "Nothing."

"Then you can give me a hand," Saint ordered. Pulling her arms free, she handed down two more flashlights to the High Wraith. Executing the same move she did earlier, she flipped her legs over and landed on the floor on the balls of her feet. Her mint green scrubs were now stained almost entirely black due to the grime in the ventilation system. Long streaks of dried blood ran down her arm and terminated at the tips of her fingers. Reaching into her pant pocket, she produced several candy bars. "I found these in the lab. It's not a lot, but at least it'll curb the hunger."

Carl started to reach for one of the bars, but Saint slapped his hand away. "I'm hungry," he protested.

"We've only been trapped down here for about half an hour," Saint pointed out as she dropped the candy back into her pocket. "You aren't starving yet."

"Candy Nazi," Carl muttered under his breath.

155

Saint ignored the comment and turned away. "We need to keep going."

CHAPTER ELEVEN

"Is anyone still alive?"

Her lonely voice echoed off the remains of the walls and floors. This place had been utterly decimated by the explosion. Entire walls had been leveled and most of the roof above had collapsed in. She had only the silvery light of the moon above her to light her way as she tried to navigate around the wreckage. The young Wraith student stumbled through what used to be the female dorms of the Academy, wearing only a tattered pair of pajama bottoms and a tank top. She had been caught sleeping by the blast. The shockwave had thrown her from bed and brought her room crashing down around her. Skittering under her bed, she had survived the collapse, but not unscathed. Her body was bruised, broken, and battered. The soles of her feet were badly cut and bleeding heavily from walking on the debris scattered around her.

Pulling her red hair from her face, she exposed a series of deep cuts down the side of her face and neck. The wound glistened from the copious amounts of Vaseline she had used to curtail the bleeding. It had been lesson one in class: vampires can smell and track even a miniscule amount of blood. Do not let a wound bleed openly. The Vaseline stung and burned against the exposed flesh, but it had to remain intact. They could be anywhere. To allow the wound to bleed was like throwing a dying seal into the midst of several white sharks. Only one thing could happen: feeding frenzy.

157

Limping forward, she stopped just outside one of the few still-standing doorframes in the hall. Glancing in, she spotted the head and torso of a teddy bear shredded on the floor. Its white stuffing was scattered around it. She suddenly felt sorry for the inanimate object. Stepping inside the room, she bent down and lifted the toy into her hands. Fear gripped her, suddenly throwing her up and back. Beneath the toy, half-buried beneath the rubble, was a bloody human arm. Turning the toy over in her hand, she saw matching bloodstains on its once soft, brown fur. As she dropped the bear to the ground, she covered her mouth and stumbled back. The urge to cry hit her hard, but she refused. As she exited the room, she tried to push the image from her mind.

She could hear the sound of water dripping in the darkness. It was deathly silent here. This place had once been a hub of life and activity, now it was a tomb. Placing her hand on a large chunk of concrete—which had formerly been part of the wall and ceiling—she stopped. Something stirred behind her. Whipping her head around, she focused her eyes into the hallway. Something was here…it made her skin crawl. Holding her breath, she took a careful step back from the concrete, her eyes firmly focused into the darkness. It felt wrong—all wrong. To be frightened in this place went against everything she knew. It was a sanctuary, a place where none of the encroaching darkness could reach or hurt her. Yet there was a snake in her garden. She could feel it slithering toward her.

Another sharp sound caught her attention. Her

head instinctively snapped in the direction of the sound. Squinting her eyes, she stared into the carcass of the hallway. Colorful bits of clothing and personal effects were in stark comparison to the flat, dark colors of the rubble, but there was no trace of whomever, or whatever, was following her. Hunting her. Drawing a forced breath, she took another step back.

It was there. She saw it.

A flash of gold shattered the darkness. Moving slowly among the rubble, she could see the outline of its body as a stream of water ran over it from a broken pipe above. It looked more like an animal than a human as it crawled through the wreckage on its hands and feet. Camouflaged, she could barely make out the details of its head and body. It looked like a smudge in the fabric of space, rather than a being. Its mental projection rippled out from a central point on its body like a pond. She knew the vampire was hunting her. She held her unblinking eyes on it as it skittered up from the floor onto what was left of the wall. It was getting closer.

A thousand things went through her mind at once. She needed to think about posture, balance, strength, and form. She was a first year student and had just begun her classes on fighting techniques and hand-to-hand combat. All of her lessons seemed to swirl in her head but created no coherent image that could help her. She would not give up, however. At least that much she remembered. She would fight until her bitter end. Finding a flat patch of ground, she spread her legs to shoulder-width, turned her body slightly against her attacker's position, and brought her balled fists up into a defensive posture. It was painfully obvious to her that this was only for show. Her muscles had no memory of the position. It felt uncomfortable and foreign to her, yet she was sure—pretty sure anyway—that this was what she was supposed to do.

She gulped hard. She was about to die and she knew it. Focusing her gaze back ahead, the hairs on the back of her neck stood up. The vampire was gone. She had violated rule number two: never take your eyes off your target. Cursing under her breath, she snapped her head around trying to reacquire her target. There was no sign of him.

Her muscles tensed. A single drop of blood ran down from her palms as her fingernails cut into her untrained flesh. Wiping them against her shirt, she took another uneasy step back. She felt something standing behind her. Before she could spin and attack, hands had been clamped around her mouth and arms. Struggling with her eyes wide, she was yanked out of the open and down toward the debris. Held firmly in position beneath an overhanging piece of concrete and rebar, she waited for death.

"Be quiet, Kara," she heard a soft voice instruct her.

Startled at hearing her name, she tried to break free. As the hand was pulled away, Kara tried to spin from the vampire's clutches. To her surprise, she saw a young woman crouched behind her. The light scar that ran down her cheek set off the dark skin of her face. "Who...?"

"Jasmine," the woman whispered quickly.

160

"Now be quiet."

Kara nodded. She had seen this woman around the dorm before. Hearing her name sparked recognition in the young woman's mind. Already having completed her tour in the field, Jasmine was waiting to take part in the ritual to make her a full Wraith. Glancing up, she surveyed their hiding spot. It was little more than an outcropping of concrete situated on a small hill of debris. It didn't hold much defensive value, but it was better than standing in the wide open bleeding. Turning, she started to slide further beneath the outcropping.

An invisible hand snapped around Kara's shoulder and ripped her from her hiding spot. Lifting the thirteen year old girl high off the ground, the vampire stared at her through golden, glowing eyes. Although still camouflaged, she could tell the monster was nearly two feet taller than her by the shape of its distortion. The student Wraith shrieked, but tried to control her fear.

"Put her down."

The vampire slowly materialized out of the ether. Augmenting its mental projection, it assumed the form of a tall, slender woman. The vampire's blond hair was wound into dozens of tight braids that hung down on all sides of her head, while her body was clad in black leather. Dark black eyeliner rimmed her eyes while her lips were painted a deep red. Her golden eyes snapped around and focused on Jasmine. Looking back to Kara, the vampire smiled and tossed the young girl away. Jasmine, dressed similarly to Kara, had crawled from beneath the outcropping and stood defiantly against the vampire. Dropping into a defensive posture, Jasmine steeled herself for the attack. She was without her scythe, and her master could not help her here. She was on her own.

"You're not even a full Wraith," the vampire scoffed. Lifting her hands up, Jasmine watched in horror as long, razor-sharp talons sprouted from the tips of her fingers.

Pressing her attack, Jasmine leapt forward. Catching her out of the air, the vampire swung Jasmine around and smashed her hard into the floor. Following her down, the creature smashed her knee directly into the center of Jasmine's spine. With a muted grunt, Jasmine rolled away from a second blow to her back. Kicking up and out, she righted herself. Throwing a punch across her body, she connected solidly with the vampire as she tried to recover. As the creature fell off balance and stumbled, Jasmine pushed herself ahead. Still bent over from the first punch, Jasmine leapt up and kicked the vampire hard in the face, knocking her back. Grabbing the back of the vampire's head, Jasmine slammed it forward into a pile of debris. Pulling it free with a handful of hair, she threw the creature's head into a solid slab of concrete.

Before the vampire could retaliate, Jasmine had backed off and returned to her defensive posture. The vampire was stronger and faster, but Jasmine had more skill. The vampire turned and stared at Jasmine with burning yellow eyes. With a shrill battle cry, the creature attacked again. Each punch, each kick, each blow was easily deflected by Jasmine. Countering another punch, Jasmine caught the vampire's arm, snapped it under her own, and brought her opposite elbow crashing down, easily breaking the bone.

Twisting her forearm down, Jasmine pinned the bloodsucker's arm behind her back. Grabbing onto the vampire's head with her free hand, she pushed the creature toward the wall. Before she hit, the creature threw her feet forward, ran up the wall and flipped over the back of Jasmine. With a laugh, she pulled her broken arm free and cracked it like a whip to reset the bone. Jasmine didn't waste any time with the antics. Punching the creature in the chin, she watched the woman stumble back. Jasmine glanced over the vampire's shoulder and smiled. Charging ahead, she jumped up and kicked the vampire directly in the center of its chest.

With a thump, the vampire fell back and suddenly stopped. Glancing down at her chest with wide eyes, the vampire saw the tip of a jagged wooden board jutting from her pale flesh. Lifting her hands to her chest, she watched the first wisps of flame flicker to life. As the flames grew in intensity, the vampire shrieked and screamed as it was engulfed. Her body writhed and seized as the blue flames quickly devoured it.

As the vampire's body crumbled to ash, red cinders flittered up and around Kara's face. Standing perfectly still with the board still in her hands, her eyes burned with satisfaction. Finally allowing herself a breath, she dropped the board to the ground and stood up.

Jasmine rushed across the floor and took the young student into her arms. "Are you okay?"

Kara said nothing, nor would she take her eyes off the pile of ashes that had just tried to kill both of them.

Jasmine forcefully lifted the young girl's face to look at her. "Kara! Are you okay?"

Kara's bottom lip quivered and her eyes welled up with tears. She quickly shook her head no.

Jasmine smiled softly and pushed the young girl's head to her shoulder. "We've got to get out of here, sweetheart."

Kara looked up at Jasmine and nodded. "Thank you."

Jasmine just smiled as she wiped Kara's tears away with her thumbs. Reaching down, she took the young Wraith by the hand and headed deeper into the Academy.

***

The massive doors of the council chamber exploded inward amidst a ball of flame and debris. Three vampires were instantly inside the darkened chamber. Standing in the moonlight that spilled in through the doors, they searched for their targets. Moving aside as if on cue, they cleared the way for a slender, robed figure. Its long shadow grew across the floor and spread into the darkness. Stepping inside the doorway, the robed figure lifted its hands and pulled the hood down revealing Brigitte's features. The dark tribal tattoo that twisted down the side of her face stood in stark comparison to her porcelain white flesh. Scanning with her glowing, golden eyes, she could see no signs of their quarry—yet they had to be there.

Lifting her hand, she snapped her fingers and motioned for her vampires to move inside. Walking deliberately through the rubble created by the exploding doors, Brigitte listened to her heels click against the concrete floor. As if she knew a secret that no one else was privy to, a soft, devious smile appeared on her face. Her cape wafted magnificently around her body as she moved. It was dark and silent. Perfect for the kill. Darkness hid a multitude of sins, yet those who committed them eventually had to face the light. She, however, did not. To her, it was all-consuming. It lifted her from normalcy and swallowed her whole. She had become the darkness.

"You might as well come out," Brigitte sang into the chamber. Her voice was light and playful, as was the mood she was in. "There's no sense in hiding."

She glanced to the left to see two of her vampires skulking through the dark. To her right, the final member of her squad skittered off the floor and onto the wall, climbing like an insect. The moonlight filtering in through the door glinted off the shiny leather of their clothes and jackets. Seeming like nothing more than ghosts in the darkness, they stalked their prey.

"I promise I'll play nice," Brigitte offered. "I won't bite," she laughed, "hard." Stopping, she ran her fingertips gently down one of the stone columns. Turning, she folded her hands neatly behind her back and rested against the mighty stone. She took a deep breath of air in through her

165

nostrils. They were here. She could taste them on the air. There was the slightest scent of ancient things mingled with the natural odor of candles and incense. Turning slightly, she saw three more vampires enter the darkened chambers and disappear into the blackness.

It was time.

Pushing off the column, Brigitte threw her cloak back over her shoulders, exposing the form-fitting black leather outfit beneath. Two long swatches of red leather sliced down the sides of her front-laced corset like two bloody fangs. At the back of the room, she spotted a white form moving in the darkness. Focusing her preternatural vision, she could make out the shape of several beings moving quickly toward the left side of the room. Snapping her fingers, she signaled her vampires and pointed out the targets. Before she had taken a step forward, she saw the first of her soldiers drop down on the elevated platform. A hissing sound was quickly silenced by the sharp sound of metal cutting through flesh. Blue flame erupted on the platform, illuminating the room. As the red cinders were tossed into the air, Brigitte caught her first full glimpse of the council members. All seven were clad in heavy white robes with their faces shadowed. She could also see a lone exit to the left that was being partially blocked by her burning soldier and another vampire perched on the wall just above it. Stepping away from the burning corpse, the seven turned and faced Brigitte.

Just as her confidence was beginning to grow, three High Wraiths materialized out of the gloom.

166

Each was dressed in the same dark coat and maroon vest and instantly snapped open their scythes and attacked. Two headed for the council, while the other leapt off the platform toward Brigitte. Catching the High Wraith in midjump, Brigitte clamped her hand around his throat and in one fluid motion, brought him over her head and crashing down into the concrete floor with a resounding crack. As his weapon skittered free of his hand, Brigitte saw a few drops of blood on the concrete behind his head. Stepping back, she watched the stunned High Wraith try and lift himself from the floor. This would be interesting.

One of Brigitte's vampires remained perched above the door to keep the council members from escaping while the other four converged on the two remaining High Wraiths. Dropping down on all sides of them, the vampires encircled the High Wraiths. Twirling their scythes furiously to create a barrier, the High Wraiths stood back-to-back. The first vampire threw himself at their opponents, his mouth wide, exposing his razor-sharp fangs. Before he could get within striking distance of the two High Wraiths, his arm had been excised and he had been knocked to the ground. Stabbing the wooden tip of his scythe into the chest of the vampire, the High Wraith pierced the vampire's heart.

Amidst the blue flames, the other vampires attacked. With his scythe still in the chest of the vampire, the High Wraith was unable to move the weapon to block. Two of the vampires latched onto their opponent and immediately started to tear at him with their claws, while the third leapt over the

167

pile and caught the other High Wraith directly in the back. Biting down on the back of his neck, the vampire latched onto several of the man's vertebrae and tore them free of his flesh. The High Wraith screamed in agony as blood sprayed in all directions. Tossing the broken spine away, the vampire stood and watched the High Wraith twitch a few times and die.

As the two High Wraiths died behind her, Brigitte advanced on the third. She could smell his blood flowing down the back of his head. She had cracked his skull against the concrete with her newly enhanced strength. The man swiped twice at Brigitte, but she easily avoided the sloppy attack. Ducking under his arms, she clasped her arms around his back and jumped high into the air. Digging her claws in, she crouched on top of the High Wraith and pinned him to the ceiling. Smashing his head to the side with her free hand, she opened her mouth wide and dug her fangs into his throat. She felt a satisfying pop as they broke through the flesh and unleashed the warm font of blood into her mouth. Pressing her lips tightly around his neck, she felt the High Wraith shiver at her touch as the tiny hairs stood up on his neck and arms. Pulling her mouth free, she swallowed the last mouthful of blood. Grabbing the High Wraith's neck, she let him fall free of the ceiling. The fall instantly snapped his neck. Tossing his limp corpse in front of the council, Brigitte dropped down gracefully in front of the platform without a sound. Drawing the back of her hand across her mouth, she smeared blood across her cheek.

"Vampire," One boomed, "you are not permitted here. For this transgression into our sacred space, you will die." Its yellow eyes glowed as brightly as Brigitte's.

"If you haven't noticed," Brigitte laughed at the threat, "we're currently kicking your ass. Your precious Academy lies in ruins and your students are dead or dying."

"Merely a setback," One assured her. "This is but one of the hundreds of academies around the globe. Our numbers are still strong." One stepped forward in the flickering light of the blue flame. "We nearly wiped your kind from the face of the Earth once and we can do it again."

Brigitte cackled. "'Nearly' being the key word in that threat." She snapped her fingers again. The remaining five vampires dropped down from their positions onto the platform around the council members. "My Lord understands there are numerous Wraith strongholds, but this is the only place in the world," Brigitte walked up the steps toward the council, but stopped just short of them, "that has the seven of you."

One suddenly saw into the depths of her plans. "You will not take us alive."

Brigitte smiled devilishly. "That was never the plan."

Launching herself forward, she caught the leader of the council flat-footed. Clawing viciously, she tore several large gashes in its robe and chest. Twisting her claws and thrusting straight up, she cut open the elder council member's throat up to his chin. His blood spilled like water from the wound.

Wrapping its pale hand over the gash, it tried to stop the bleeding, but it was too severe. The deep red liquid poured through One's fingers. Staring at the vampire in awe, its gold eyes dimmed slightly. Taking a breath, the elder crumbled to the floor. Brigitte slowly turned her gaze to the remaining six members of the council.

***

Saint had fallen to the back of the group and was warily eying Xavier. At the head of the line, the High Wraith was moving carefully, but quickly through the damaged halls. He danced lightly around the piles of rubble, his dark coat billowing behind him like a cape. From the way he held his body to the way his feet fell to the floor, he felt wrong to Saint. From her earliest days at the Academy, she had seen how the High Wraiths moved, their posture, and how they maintained themselves. They were the best of the best and most presented themselves as such. This man didn't seem to possess any of that. From his unwillingness to take leadership of the group, to his lackadaisical treatment of the two technicians, this man didn't portray himself as a Master Wraith. Saint would have to keep a watchful eye on this man. He was not what he appe—

"Can I have one of those candy bars now?"

Saint snapped her attention back to the group. "What?"

Carl stopped and turned to the Saint. "The candy you have in your pocket. Can I have one now?"

Saint shot a cross look at the man. "Why are you so insistent on getting one? We haven't been down here more than two hours yet."

"I'm hypoglycemic," Carl spat quickly.

"So sugar would be the worst thing for you right now," Saint countered. "Right?"

Carl's face twisted as he tried to come up with another line. After a moment, a defeated look appeared. "I'm just hungry," he admitted.

"So I've heard," Saint laughed. Looking past Carl and Mark, her eyes hardened. "Where's Xavier?"

Mark and Carl quickly spun and stared into the darkness where the High Wraith had previously been standing. No sign of his flashlight beam could be seen. Listening into the void, Saint could detect no footsteps or the telltale swish of cloth that would identify him.

Saint moved passed the two technicians and quickly swept her light over the corridor. "What the hell?" she muttered. "Did either of you see where he went?"

The two techs quickly shook their heads.

"Xavier?" Saint called into the dark. A lump formed in her throat but quickly sank down into the bottom of her stomach. "Xavier?"

"Maybe he fell," Mark suggested, "or something."

"Yeah," Carl interjected, "maybe he's hurt and can't reply."

Saint scowled. "Not a High Wraith." Running the white beam of her flashlight over the nearby debris, she looked for any signs that the High Wraith had fallen or gotten trapped somehow. She saw three large piles directly in front of her position, each threatening at any moment to tumble and completely block the hallway. Portions of the roof had collapsed in, revealing the level above them. She could easily make the jump, but the two techs would not.

"People just don't disappear," Mark stated.

"Wraiths can," Saint shot back, "and vampires." Her response was dripping with venom and disdain.

Mark stood in shock staring at Saint. "What are you trying to say?"

Saint turned slowly back to the two techs. "I'm only making a point," she added quickly.

"I don't really care if that guy's gone," Carl said as he put another cigarette in his mouth. "He gives me the jibblies. I hope he fell down a huge hole to his death." Leaning over, he lit his cigarette.

"That's lovely," Mark said angrily. "Are you naturally this charming?"

"As a matter of fact, I am," Carl said as he blew smoke from his nose. "I just don't like him," he defended. "He can go see the horned one, for all I care."

"Shut up," Saint said, waving her hand at the two. Taking a step away from the bickering pair, she perked her ears. She could detect the faint sound of scraping in the blackness. Moving another step ahead, she tried to home in on the sound. It sounded like someone walking on gravel. Working back uneasily, Saint snapped off her light and quickly instructed the other two to do the same. Pushing back against the wall, she tried to focus her eyes. She could see a faint glow from the floor above through one of the holes. The sudden flash of light seemed to draw all of the air out of the room as she unconsciously began to hold her breath. Holding her position, she trained her eyes on the light, forcing her eyes not to blink.

She could hear the breathing of the two techs beside her become quick and shallow as they fed off each other's fear. This was the worst kind of situation Saint told herself. As they struggled toward the surface, they had no idea of its condition or what had actually happened. They could be rushing blindly into another disaster. She saw the light flash through the hole and down over the rubble in front of them. Two feet to the left, and they might have seen an arm or leg in the light. Gritting her teeth, Saint held her position. As the loudness of the sound increased, she balled up her fists. She saw a form silhouetted by the flashlight leap down through the hole. Dropping her shoulder, she charged forward and hit the figure squarely in the back. As the two spilled to the floor, she heard a familiar voice.

"Wait, stop!"

Saint pulled back, surprised. "Miller?"

Miller rolled onto his back and shined his light into the face of his attacker. "Saint?"

Reaching forward, Saint grabbed the Wraith by his collar and pulled him into a tight embrace. "I'm so glad you're here," she said, losing herself. As his hands wrapped around her back, a sudden feeling of

173

paranoia gripped her. Pulling free of the hug, she looked into the face of her best friend. "What are you doing here?"

Miller took a deep breath. "I was heading back from my first assignment from the council and I saw the explosion."

Saint looked at him quizzically. "Explosion?"

"You don't know?"

"We've all been stuck down here since before everything went to hell," she confessed.

"I don't know specific details," Miller admitted, "but I saw a massive explosion rip through the Academy." A faraway look passed over his face. "It was horrible. I saw Wraiths burning in the street," he paused, "and others who weren't so lucky."

Saint clamped her hand over her mouth. "Who did this?"

"I don't know," Miller said quickly. "I only know that in the aftermath, the Academy has been overrun by vampires. They're everywhere."

"That's it," Carl shouted from the back of the group. Rushing toward Saint, he grabbed her shoulders and pulled one of the candy bars free of her pocket. "If I'm going to die," he said, tearing off the wrapper, "I'm going to have a fucking candy bar." Taking a large bite of the chocolate and caramel, he sighed with pleasure. "Oh, yeah."

Saint made no move to stop the cranky tech, or to reprimand him. Turning her attention back to Miller, a curious look crossed her face. "I have to go back to my original question, what are you doing here?" Her tone turned quickly cold.

174

Miller looked oddly at Saint. "After I saw the vampires moving inside, I snuck in to try and help any survivors I could find," he defended. "Why are you treating me this way?"

Saint looked for a long time at her beau, then sighed. Pulling a bit of hair from her face, she placed a hand on his shoulder, "I'm sorry. I'm just a little on edge," she said, refusing to even acknowledge the grief she was still swimming in. "I'm getting a whole 'I Am Legend' vibe."

Miller nodded. "I haven't come across a lot of survivors."

"You haven't found anyone on the upper levels?" Mark cut in.

"No," Miller said slowly, "I didn't say that. I haven't found any survivors."

"Oh," Mark breathed.

"We need to get you three out of here," Miller said after a long pause. "I ran across several vampires on the next level up a while back. There were too many. I couldn't attack."

Saint took a long look at the two frightened techs standing behind her. Her eyes fell on the young face of Mark. He was only her age, but unlike her, he wasn't here to fight. He hadn't chosen to be a part of this war and yet he was stuck in the middle of it. She had to get them out of here, yet one question remained. "We can't leave."

"Why?" Miller asked.

"We're short one man," Saint replied. "We had a High Wraith with us, Xavier. He just," she paused, "vanished."

"Xavier," Miller said, rolling the name around

in his mouth. "Doesn't sound familiar."

"I know," Saint nodded, "but we can't leave without him."

Miller smiled and patted his best friend on the shoulder. "We'll find your missing High Wraith."

CHAPTER TWELVE

Standing in the open, Bane scanned the complex. He felt no danger, no need to haunt the shadows as some of his soldiers did. He was a powerful and proud warrior. To be forced to using explosive devices hindered his pride slightly, but in war, honor was often the first thing abandoned. His hatred of this place and those it contained was all-consuming. So much so, the blood burned in his veins as he stood in the ruins of it. They had done this to him, and they would be made to pay...dearly. Even if he had to tear each and every Wraith in this place limb from limb with his own decaying hands, he would do so to ensure it would never attain its former glory again.

Taking a step forward, he took a deep whiff of the acrid smoke that hung in the air. It was the smell of impending death, and Bane enjoyed it. Snapping open his arm blades, he tossed his cape back and marched further into the complex. Walking through flame and debris, his ears detected the faint sound of footsteps. Stopping, he quieted his body and listened. They were moving toward him, yet they were—he paused and cocked his head slightly—below his position. Closing his eyes for a moment, he knelt down and pressed his hand to the concrete floor. Amidst the constant odor of smoke, he could detect the faintest odor of humans. He took another whiff, and slowly opened his eyes. There were four of them, and two were Wraiths. Standing, Bane smiled. One of the Wraiths was slightly different than the others. He couldn't be sure yet, but this could present a new wrinkle in his plans. He was, of course, familiar with the tales and legends, but could it be true? A devious smile spread across his face.

Leaping up, he shot off into the darkness. His targets had been acquired and nothing would keep him from them.

***

Lifting the bottom of her dirty shirt, Saint wrapped her hands around the fabric and tied it into a knot, exposing her toned midriff. Running her grimy hands through her raven hair, she tried to smooth it back to her head, but it was no use. It had developed a will of its own since her last shower. Glancing ahead, she tried to see the others. She had been flanking the group for some time as Miller had taken the lead and she'd lost track of them. Not overly concerned as Miller was with them, she nevertheless, needed to catch up. There was, of course, safety in numbers. She would not be responsible for any more deaths.

Moving quickly down the damaged hall, she heard a small splash as she stepped forward. Stopping again, she knelt down and saw the puddle of water forming on the floor. Setting her light on the floor, she pointed it at the wall. Reaching over, she pressed her hand flat to the darkened area and felt a cool stream of water running over her fingers. With a sigh of relief, she placed both hands in the leak and let the coolness relax her for a moment. Lifting her arm, she stared at the long gash she had created in the vent shaft. The exposed tin had easily sliced open her arm. A normal human would require stitches to properly heal, but Saint wasn't exactly human anymore. The wound had already begun to scab over and heal. Pulling away, she shook her hands of the excess water and stood up.

Her mind swam in the darkness that surrounded her. Her thoughts turned again to the missing High Wraith, but began to shift back to Master Quinn. Guilt clung to her like wet clothes. If only she had been there for him. She tried to tell herself it wasn't her fault, but she had already convinced herself otherwise. Not even knowing what or who had claimed his life, Saint knew she could have helped. In the five years the two had spent together, he had never received anything deadlier than a scratch. Now he was dead and she had failed him. She wanted him here right now. She wanted him to place his strong hands on her shoulders, look into her eyes, and tell her everything was going to be okay. She desperately needed that. To hear his voice just one last time... He was her safety blanket, the net to catch her if she fell. Now she was alone for the very first time in her life. She was on her own. She couldn't tell if she was missing her master, or just feeling sorry for herself. Guilt complicated the issue.

A scream in the darkness snapped her mind back to reality. Hardening her eyes, she charged recklessly into the all-consuming blackness toward the source of the sound. Leaping over shoulder-high piles of debris with the ease of an Olympic athlete, Saint flew through the hallway. Ahead of her, she

179

could finally make out the glare of the group's flashlights. One was stationary on the floor while the other two seemed to be moving frantically about the enclosed space. Clicking off her own light, she carefully traversed the final few meters silently. Coming up on her group, she could only see two figures standing in the dark.

Scanning the scene, Saint couldn't detect the source of the scream. Moving into the light, she looked at Miller and then Carl. "What the hell's going on here?"

Miller turned to see Saint for the first time. His eyes were wide with shock. "I honestly don't know," he breathed. "I turned and saw—"

"Something fucking grabbed Mark!" Carl shouted frantically. Grabbing onto Saint's shoulders, he stared angrily into her eyes. "It reached out of the shadows and took him!"

"Who?" Saint asked, easily breaking free of his grasp. "Who took Mark?"

"Who do you fucking think?" Carl growled.

"Vampires?" Saint asked, turning to Miller.

Miller nodded slowly, the look of shock still firmly fixed on his face. "I didn't see anything as I walked by," he said, pointing to a gaping hole in the wall. A few twisted strands of rebar sprouted from the concrete like ribs jutting from a chest wound. "But it just jumped out and grabbed him."

"It's like some demonic whack-a-mole game," Carl shouted, obviously so frightened, his mind was going into shock.

"Did you get a good look?" Saint asked, ignoring Carl.

180

Miller shook his head.

Saint pulled a quick breath into her lungs. Without another second of hesitation, Saint pushed open Miller's coat, snatched his scythe and tossed him her flashlight. Turning away from the others, Saint clutched the mystical weapon tightly in her fist and charged toward the hole. Grabbing the exposed rebar, she swung herself inside and crouched down. Focusing all of her preternatural vision, she scanned the area. The hole led directly into an adjoining chamber. Several large chunks of the roof had fallen in, exposing the room above as well. Slowly standing, Saint kept to the wall and began to circle the room. There were several tall glass cylinders on the far side, only one of which wasn't broken. It contained a greenish liquid with lights in the bottom and was casting an ominous glare over the room.

Stepping over a fallen file cabinet, Saint stopped. There, on the far side of the room just below the last remaining intact tube was Mark. Holding the scythe tightly, she charged across the room, fear in her heart. He wasn't moving. Dropping down to her knees, she skidded to a stop next to his body. Grabbing his head, she turned it to the side exposing a gaping bite wound in his throat. Gritting her teeth, she let his head fall back and slowly lowered his eyelids. He was already gone. Standing up, she activated Miller's scythe. As the large blade sprouted from the top of the scythe, she brought it down quickly and severed Mark's head to ensure that he didn't return. She took a step away from the body while shaking her head. He didn't deserve this.

"I see you, Wraith," a voice hissed from somewhere in the room.

Saint's muscles instantly tensed. Holding the weapon tightly, she snapped her head up and scanned the room. Beyond the green glow of the tube, there was no sign of the vampire. "Come out where I can see you," Saint said slowly. "It's only fair."

Silence.

Saint walked slowly back toward the center of the room. This wasn't an ideal place for a battle. There was no space to maneuver. She could easily become trapped. "Coward," she goaded, "you won't even show your face to a harmless little woman?"

"Your friend tasted sweet," the vampire hissed again, overexaggerating the "s" sounds in his sentences.

Saint whipped her head up toward the ceiling. Through the gaping scar, she thought she spotted the creature. Closing her eyes, she reached out with her senses. As they crept over the debris and cracks, her eyes suddenly snapped open. "Shit," she muttered quickly.

Charging forward, she placed her foot on a bit of fallen roof and launched herself up through the hole in the ceiling. Flipping in the air, she came down perfectly on the balls of her feet and immediately ripped the scythe across her body. Blue flame erupted out of the darkness accompanied by a horrible shriek. The vampire's mental projection quickly began to fail. It shimmered into existence just as the last of the blue flame engulfed its body. Twisting the scythe in her hands, she stabbed the wooden tip straight back behind her. Feeling it impact firmly, she smiled. Looking over her shoulder, she saw another vampire burning to ash. Ripping the weapon free of the creature's dying form, she spun it in a flourish above her head and crouched down into a defensive position. Looking around the room, she saw several more vampires materialize out of the gloom like apparitions.

Saint looked slowly over each of her opponents. "Who's next?"

Standing around the hole in the ceiling, each of the six vampires remained motionless. Their golden eyes remained fixed on her.

"Come on!" Saint shouted. "Who wants some of this?"

As if on cue, the vampires melted back into the darkness. Whipping the scythe around her body, Saint flung it hard across the room to where one of the vampires had just been standing. To her surprise, she hit nothing. The scythe impacted the wall and clattered to the floor. Instantly retracting into its compact form, it rolled silently toward the corner. Standing straight, Saint searched the room with her senses.

Cocking her head slightly, she ran around the edge of the room and retrieved Miller's scythe. Leaping into the air, she sailed down through the hole back into the room below. Glancing at Mark's body one final time, she ducked through the hole in the wall to rejoin Miller and Carl. Standing, she tossed the weapon back to Miller.

"Did you find him?" Carl asked impatiently.

Saint nodded. "I'm sorry."

Carl lifted his head and spun on his heels. Balling his fists, he roared into the darkness at the top of his lungs.

Miller placed a hand on Saint's shoulder. "Did you see the vampire?"

She brushed off his hand. Grabbing him by the arm, she forcefully pulled him away from Carl. "What were you doing?" Her voice was low and angry.

"What?" Miller asked quickly. "What are you talking about?"

Saint glared at him. She had no time for excuses. "Were you spacing off? Or just not paying attention to the people in your care?"

Miller's expression turned angry. "I don't think I like your attitude. That vampire grabbed him so fast, I didn't have a chance to react."

"Bullshit," Saint spat. "I had time to catch up with you guys and you stood there doing nothing. If anything," she added, "you should have been right in that hole after the vampire. You might've been able to catch him and save Mark."

"Might have," Miller echoed. "There's nothing that—"

"Don't even finish that sentence," she growled. "You froze, plain and simple."

Miller steeled himself for a fight. "Who the fuck put you in charge anyway?"

"You did," she replied calmly, "when you did nothing."

"Is this some kind of woman thing I should know about?" Miller spat, "because if it's that time of the month or something, you really should tell me."

Saint slapped Miller hard across the face, knocking him to the ground. "How dare you trivialize this? A man is dead because of you!" Grabbing him by the collar, she easily lifted him off the ground. Spinning around, she slammed him hard against the wall. "If you're not with us," she looked at him for a long moment, "you're against us. Which is it?"

Miller tried to break her grip, but couldn't. She was the stronger of the two. He felt a giant welt forming on his face where she had slapped him. He looked into the steely gray eyes of his best friend and suddenly became afraid. In the pools where he had once seen passion and life, now only pain existed. She was hurting inside and she was going to let anyone who stood in her way be her release. Even him. He suddenly felt sorry for her. Lifting his hands away from her, he held up his palms, surrendering. "With you," he said after a moment. "Of course, I'm with you."

Her stare was unwavering. Slowly, she relaxed her grip and let go. Taking a deep breath, she stepped away from Miller into the darkness. Lifting her head, she ran her fingers slowly through her hair.

Miller adjusted his coat and quickly turned back to Carl, who was standing awestruck after seeing the confrontation between the two. "Are you okay?"

Carl shook his head. "No, but you don't look so well either. That handprint on your face is brighter than Rudolph's nose."

Miller lifted his hand and slowly ran his fingertips across it. His cheek throbbed and radiated pain out in all directions.

"Why did she do that?" Carl asked.

"I deserved it," Miller defended Saint. "I was being careless."

"In my day," Carl smirked, "we didn't let our women behave like that. Although," he leaned over slightly and stared at Saint, "that one could probably break both of us in half like sticks. Right?"

Miller, his hand pressed to the mark on his face, nodded.

"Enough said," Carl nodded. "Let's get the hell out of here. I don't want to wait around just in case one of those things comes back."

Miller understood. Turning, he looked at Saint. "Are you ready?"

Saint turned to see both Miller and Carl staring at her. Taking a quick breath, she forced a smile. "Let's get going."

***

Jasmine and Kara tried to be as silent as possible as they moved through the Academy's ruins. Further away from the epicenter of the blast, the damage wasn't as bad. Walking briskly through the mostly intact halls of the east wing, they were heading toward the council chambers. It was the

186

only place either of the girls assumed would be safe in a crisis such as this. Numerous High Wraiths guarded the council. This led them to suspect there would still be help there in one form or another. It was all they had.

Limping, Kara had her arm around Jasmine's shoulders for support. Her feet were a road map of lacerations, blood, and bruises. With each step, it became harder and harder to continue on. As each foot fell, she couldn't help but whimper as a shock of pain shot up her legs. Jasmine wasn't faring much better, but she had to remain strong for Kara's sake. The two were depending on each other.

Kara was a first year student with very little knowledge and experience under her belt, while Jasmine was as close to being a Wraith as possible without actually having gone through the ritual. Both had scythes, but they had been lost or dropped in the confusion of the moment. To Kara, the scythe was little more than a token representation of what she would eventually become, but to Jasmine, it had become an extension of herself. She cursed under her breath for losing it. That was a rookie mistake, and reinforced in her mind why she had not been chosen to participate in this year's ritual.

Stopping for a breather, Jasmine looked up to see the entrance to the council chambers just ahead. The scene was somehow wrong though. Everything was in place, but the chamber doors were wide open. In her ten years at the Academy, she had never seen them open like that. Something wasn't right.

"I need you to stay here," Jasmine said quietly. Moving toward the closest wall, she sat the student Wraith down on one of the benches scattered around the lobby. Squatting down, she placed her hand on Kara's knee. "Are you going to be okay by yourself for a minute?"

Kara nodded bravely, even though she didn't want to be left behind. It did feel good to take the weight off her battered feet though. "Do what you need to do," she said quickly. "I'll be right here when you get back."

Jasmine smiled. Reaching up, she patted Kara on the shoulder. Standing, she turned and stared at the entrance to the council chambers. Moving across the cold floor on her bare feet, she listened to her footsteps pop lightly in the silence. Pressing her back to the wall just beyond the door, Jasmine looked carefully around the lobby for any other signs of a struggle. Spotting two red banners hanging on the wall, she found what she had been seeking. Both of the banners were shredded about halfway down, leaving only tattered rags wafting gently in the breeze that seemed to be emanating from the open chambers.

Scooting closer to the door, Jasmine perked her ears and listened inside. She detected the faint sound of footsteps, and what sounded to her like something being dragged. Wrapping her fingertips gently around the doorframe, she recoiled quickly at the prick of sharp splinters jutting out in all directions. Her sense of dread doubled almost instantly. Looking across to the opposite side of the frame, she could see it had been shredded. A few of

188

the heavy hinges still clung uselessly in place. Several large chunks of wood littered the floor around the doorway, signaling to Jasmine that the doors had been forcefully taken down. Leaning her head back against the wall for a moment, she swallowed a breath and realized that her and Kara's salvation was not to be found here.

Mustering her courage, she peered around the broken doorframe into the council chambers. She had only stood in this place twice before in her time at the Academy. Both were instances when the High Council was judging her on performances. The second was when she found out that she would not be participating in the ritual to make her a full Wraith this year. It had been a major blow to her ego, but in the end, she understood. Her master had gone to great lengths to teach her humility. She was well aware that she needed more training, the scar on her face reminded her of that daily. She would eventually receive the ritual—of this she was certain—but it would take more hard work and dedication.

The room was bathed in the golden glow from dozens of candles, but there was no warmth. The chamber felt cold and hard, like a mausoleum. The stone pillars arranged through the room stood silently, unable to reveal the events that had befallen this place. At the head of the room, Jasmine looked over the raised platform and wide stairs. Two bodies were there. Focusing her eyes, she caught a glimpse of the red vests each wore. She felt her heart drop down into her stomach with a thump. There, leaning in the corner of the room, was a vampire. He was preoccupied with cleaning his fingernails of whatever grime he had accumulated there, ignoring all else. She watched two more vampires emerge from a door on the far side of the platform. One was the standard goon dressed totally in black leather with more tattoos on its body than clothes, while the other was tall, thin, and completely swathed in a heavy, black robe. Jasmine watched the robed vampire walk across the platform quickly and strike the vampire who had been cleaning his nails across the face. Jasmine edged close to the door and tried to make out their conversation.

"Mistress," the vampire recoiled, dropping his nail file to the floor, "what have I done?"

The robed vampire glared down at her subject. "You were sloppy. You cost us the lives of a soldier with your incompetence."

Sinking down to his knees, he cowered slightly. He lifted his hands and surrendered to the robed vampire. "I apologize, Mistress Brigitte. The High Wraith were many," he tried to explain.

Brigitte lifted her hand to strike the soldier again.

"We eliminated the council," he pleaded, turning his face away, whimpering like a coward. "We achieved Lord Bane's goal."

Jasmine's mouth fell agape in horror.

"We did," Brigitte breathed. She let her hand fall back to her side. "Understand this," she growled at her subject, "you are to be punished when we are finished here. But until then, I still need you," she said begrudgingly. "Stand up and

190

act like a real soldier. Show some dignity. You are a soldier in Lord Bane's army."

The vampire quickly complied.

"We all are," Brigitte said, addressing her subjects. "We have done the unthinkable. We have destroyed the Wraith single-handedly. For this, you will all be rewarded."

Her vampires roared in approval.

"But first," she said with a smirk, "there's more work to be done." Brigitte turned toward the mouth of the chamber and stopped.

Jasmine ripped her head from the doorway. Pressing herself to the wall, her palms were wet with sweat. Had she been spotted? She tried to gain control of her body and listen again. She heard nothing from inside the chamber. After what seemed like an eternity, Jasmine finally pulled herself away from the wall and turned back toward the door. Placing her hand gently on the frame, she swallowed hard and began to lean over.

A ghostly white hand shot from the darkness and clamped around Jasmine's throat. Fighting and kicking against the unseen enemy, Jasmine felt her feet leave the floor. As her airway was slowly crushed under her own weight, her eyes rolled down to see Brigitte standing before her. The vampire's eyes were burning in her pale face as she sneered at the student Wraith.

Holding Jasmine high off the floor, Brigitte exposed her fangs. "We have a little chocolate spy," she laughed. Taking a deep whiff of the Wraith, the vampire frowned in disappointment. "Not a Wraith. Just scared out of your wits. Who are you?"

191

Jasmine choked and gagged as she tried to draw breath. She clawed against the vampire's hand.

"Not talking?" Brigitte laughed, "That's okay. I've developed a real talent for torture lately."

Jasmine's eyes darted to the side, then quickly back to Brigitte.

Brigitte watched the young student with pleasure. "What is it, little one?" She peered past Jasmine to see Kara curled up in the corner behind a tall plant. "You brought me another one? How thoughtful of you."

"Kara," Jasmine managed to shout, "run!"

Kara jumped up from her position and stared anxiously toward the council chambers. Seeing the vampire pinning Jasmine to the wall, she immediately turned and began to run as fast as she could. Hobbling on her battered feet, she couldn't hit top speed.

"That isn't playing nice," Brigitte said with a frown. "You have to be punished now." Squeezing her hand, she crushed Jasmine's windpipe. Dropping the girl to the ground, she watched her flop, gasp, and writhe like a fish out of water. "Oh for fuck's sake," Brigitte said with an air of boredom and anger, "Just die already." Grabbing Jasmine's hair, she lifted the girl up and bit into her throat.

Kara glanced over her shoulder one last time to see the vampire sucking Jasmine's blood. Nausea washed over her at the sight and tears instantly began to stream down her face. Turning away, she gritted her teeth and forced herself to focus.

Jasmine had bought her time to escape with her life. She wouldn't let that sacrifice be in vain. Pushing off the wall, she turned and ran into the darkness.

CHAPTER THIRTEEN

Amidst the burning wreckage and debris, two men stood in tattered clothing. Each was rugged and well-built, but they looked as if their bodies hadn't touched water in some time. Their gaunt faces were smeared with dirt and grime as they looked over the wreckage. Their eyes told their story: shock and dismay at the scene. Walking slowly over the battlefield, they carefully avoided the bodies out of respect for the fallen warriors. They had never witnessed destruction of this magnitude. In the long and guarded history of this order, a massacre of this scale had never been recorded. The two men looked to each other.

"Why were we not called?"

The second man looked over the wreckage knowingly. "They did not have time. This was a quick, surgical strike. The order was caught unaware."

The first man furrowed his brow and nodded at the assessment. "We are too late."

"No," the first man corrected him. Lifting his head, he sniffed the air. Amidst the smell of smoke and burning flesh, he detected living creatures. "We can still help."

Patting his friend on the back, the men turned and charged into the Academy. They could not become preoccupied with the dead while there were still living souls to be tended to. That was their pledge to these people, and they would not default on it now. There was too much at stake.

The water around their feet had steadily begun to increase as they moved further into the darkness. From a few puddles, it had was now well above their knees. The cold water was bone chilling. Already, high tensions were threatening to boil over at any moment as they trudged through. It also made seeing debris on the floor much more difficult and had slowed their progress. Still in the lead, Saint waved her flashlight over the hallway and down into the water trying to avoid obstacles. Her hand firmly on the wall next to her, she tried to retain her balance as she moved. The sloshing and echoing of the water voided any chance they had of a silent escape. Looking back, she saw that Carl was right behind her, a slightly soggy cigarette hanging out of his mouth. Miller had fallen back to the rear of the group making sure not to look directly at Saint.

A slight twinge of guilt gnawed at her. She shouldn't have been so hard on Miller, but someone had died on his watch. Of course, there was plenty of blame to go around. Instead of keeping up with the group, she had lagged behind and become embroiled in her own depression. Had she been there, she knew she could have saved Mark, but in the few seconds it took her to act and close the distance with the others, she had lost him. Reaching down, she cupped her hand and lifted a handful of the cold water. Splashing it on her face, she tried to push the grief and guilt away.

Squinting her eyes, she could see a dim light at

the end of the hall. Pausing for a moment, she waited for the others to catch up. She snapped off her flashlight. Staring ahead, she hoped the light hadn't been a reflection from any of their flashlights. As her light quickly faded, she was relieved to see the glow remain. She couldn't quite tell what it was, but it seemed to be emanating from the top of the hall, rather than from beneath the water. Reaching back, she pulled Carl next to her and pointed down the hall. "What do you see?"

"Is this some kind of trick question?" Carl said gruffly, trying to keep his wet cigarette lit. He had stumbled over a large chunk of wreckage about ten minutes ago and fallen head first into the water. His entire pack was drenched, despite the cellophane it was wrapped in. Pulling the cigarette from his mouth, he tossed it angrily into the water. "All I see is water and more water."

"No," Saint said, trying to be patient, "look there."

Carl followed her finger toward a glare further down the hall. "I see it. What the hell is it?"

Saint bit her bottom lip, careful not to puncture it with her new fangs. "I don't know. Could be anything." She turned to see Miller finally catch up. "Do you see a light down there?"

Miller leaned forward slightly and narrowed his eyes. "I think so. Hard to tell though."

Saint nodded. "I'm going to take a look."

"What about the rest of us?" Carl protested, obviously afraid to be left alone with Miller.

"I'll be faster on my own," Saint argued. "I won't be gone long."

"Sure," Carl breathed, "You say that now."

Saint ignored Carl's comment. She looked up to Miller. "Keep an eye on things, will you?"

Miller nodded once.

Turning away from the other two, Saint started deeper into the numbingly cold water. Holding her flashlight at the ready, she realized she couldn't feel her feet anymore. Clicking her thumb over the flashlight's activation switch, she breathed a little easier as the white glow filled the hallway. Moving ahead, she felt the water rise again. It was at her hips now, threatening to engulf her entire body at any moment. Stepping on the large outcroppings of debris, she tried to get above the water. Moving quickly now, she could clearly see an illumination at the end. It was little more than a hole in the ceiling with a bright light shining down. Moving under the hole, she peered through. Several large floodlights seemed to have been placed around the area above. Shielding her eyes for a moment, she saw a welcome relief: stars glittering above. They had made it out.

Turning back, she placed her fingers in her mouth and whistled loudly. Waving with her arm, she motioned for Carl and Miller to join her.

The ceiling was roughly ten feet high. A very difficult reach for a human, but for a Wraith, it was no problem. Positioning her legs on a nearby pile of wreckage, she leapt straight up through the hole. Coming down, she widened her legs to catch both sides with her feet. Jumping back, she stopped and quickly surveyed the Academy. To her horror, it was merely a shell of its former self. Whatever had

197

happened up here, it looked as if it had claimed most of the main building and large portions of the west wing. Very little remained that would identify it as the Wraith Academy. It reminded her of pictures she had seen on the news of the World Trade Center buildings in New York after the terrorist attacks on September 11th. It had been completely decimated.

Turning back to the scar in the ground, she dropped down to her knees and peered inside. Below, she could clearly see Carl and Miller. "Lift him up, Miller," Saint instructed. "I'll pull him free."

Miller took a step forward and grabbed Carl's waist. "That isn't necessary."

With one quick motion, he had flung the man straight into the air. Carl screamed as he sailed past Saint. Falling down hard on the far side of the hole, Carl crumbled to the ground with a thud. Saint was quickly up and at his side. "Are you okay?"

"Did you get the name of that truck?" Carl asked with a groan. Falling back, he grabbed his knees and quickly began rubbing them.

Saint looked over her shoulder angrily at Miller who had just leapt free of the hole as well. Gritting her teeth, she felt her fangs dig into the soft, pink flesh of her gums. This wasn't the man she knew. Standing up, she tossed her flashlight down and walked slowly toward Miller. "What the hell was that?"

"I just tossed him free," Miller said with a grin. "Gave me a chance to use these new powers of mine."

That settled it. No Wraith ever bragged about their powers. This wasn't Miller Barnes.

Charging forward, Saint lowered her shoulder and slammed into Miller's midsection. The two Wraiths tumbled back and fell through the hole again. Splashing down hard into the water and debris below, Saint was the first back on her feet. She watched Miller lift his head from the water, gasping for breath. Maneuvering a few steps away from him, Saint readied herself.

"I don't know who the hell you are," Saint warned, "but just because you have Miller's face, doesn't mean I'll show you any mercy."

Miller's face was full of confusion. "Saint, what is this? You know me, you've known me since you were thirteen."

"You're not Miller Barnes," Saint said, balling her fists. Lunging forward, she caught Miller flat-footed and delivered a heavy right hook across his chin. Reversing her attack, she brought her elbow back and slammed it into his eye socket.

Miller fell back into the water again. Pushing himself away from Saint, he glared angrily at her. "Your favorite artist is the Cure," he said quickly. "You love the song Every Breath You Take, and your favorite beer is Guinness."

"That doesn't prove anything," Saint said, moving toward Miller. "Anyone could know that." She lifted the wet Wraith from the water with one arm and pinned him against the wall. "Try again."

Miller's head fell back for a minute as he searched his mind. "When we were talking about leaving the Academy, your Master caught us.

199

Quinn told us that we would not only be shaming the Academy, but ourselves if we left. We had our duties to think about, rather than the animal lust in our hearts."

Saint paused. Only three people in the world knew of that conversation, and one of them was dead.

"He told you to think with your head," Miller recalled, "not with your pants."

Saint let her hand slip away from Miller. She took a step back and looked at him oddly. "What happened to you?"

"I met a man on my first mission," Miller said, adjusting his coat. "He taught me the true way of the world."

Saint was at a complete loss. "Who was this man?"

A slow grin crossed Miller's face. "Can't ruin the surprise."

Saint's body suddenly went on alert again. "What?"

Miller jumped forward and tackled Saint. As the two fell into the water, his hands slipped around her throat. He would drown her. Struggling beneath the water, Saint tried to get control of her panicking body. Grabbing onto Miller's hands, she tried to pull them free, but it was no use. He was indeed powerful now, but not as strong as she was. Saint's hand shot out of the water and snapped around Miller's throat. Lurching forward, she lifted herself and Miller away from the water. Rage gripped her as she stared at his face. Whipping him across her body, she slammed his head into the wall and let

200

go. The Wraith stumbled back, dazed.

"You are not Miller Barnes," Saint growled. "I'll kill you for even trying to impersonate him."

Miller reached up and ran his fingers through the gushing blood on his forehead. With a snicker, he wiped it away. With an evil grin, he dropped down into a defensive position and raised his fists. "Bring it on, bitch."

Saint screamed and charged. As the two powerful combatants met, the water exploded around them. Each holding their position, they delivered blow after blow to the face and body of their opponent. They stood toe-to-toe, just pounding on each other and taking the abuse. Neither would budge, neither would fall. Finally, Miller dodged Saint's punch and ducked into her body. Leaning in, he jabbed her once right above the pubic area. As Saint gasped in pain, Miller straightened up, giving her a reverse head butt that caught her just below her chin. Her head was snapped straight back. Pushing his advantage, Miller flattened his hand and jabbed his fingertips hard into the center of Saint's windpipe. The Wraith stumbled back, her hand instantly clasping around her throat.

Miller walked slowly around her, adjusting his coat. "You're more important than you think," he said after a moment. "There was a prophecy written about you nearly five thousand years ago. I don't know what it says exactly, but my new master says it determines your fate," he smiled, "and ours."

Saint glared at Miller. "How can you do this?" she croaked. "You are a Wraith."

"I had a change of heart," Miller admitted. "I

was sent here to get you, to bring you to him. And that's exactly what I'm going to do. I—" Miller gasped as a sharp pain tore through his back.

"I don't think that's the case."

Saint looked up to see Xavier standing behind Miller. Xavier's scythe was firmly embedded in Miller's back. Pulling it free, he spun it around his body and brought it horizontally across Miller's body, easily chopping the Wraith in half.

Saint watched the two pieces of Miller slump forward into the water with a splash. Fear, anger, and pain gripped her body. Falling down to her knees, she balled her fists as her body shook. It wasn't Miller she tried to tell herself as his blood began to mingle in the water around her. It wasn't Miller.

Xavier snapped his scythe closed and reattached it to his belt. Stepping past the corpse, he stopped in front of Saint and extended his hand. "I'm sorry I didn't get here sooner."

Saint was bordering on a state of shock as she accepted his hand and stood up. She couldn't seem to get her eyes to come away from the body in front of her.

Xavier leaned closer to the young woman to try and get her attention. "Saint?"

She continued to stare at the blood diffusing around her feet.

"Saint!" Xavier grabbed her face and forcefully turned it toward him. Her gray eyes were wide with guilt and anguish. "Pull it together," he commanded.

"He," she felt the words drowning in her throat,

202

"he was my best friend."

"That wasn't your friend anymore," the High Wraith confirmed. "He had become an agent of our enemy. His will was not his own."

"How do you know?" Saint asked pleadingly, looking for any shred of reason or proof that could pull her back from this pit of darkness she was descending into.

"He jumped me earlier," Xavier admitted. "I had gotten a little ahead of the group and he made his move. He used some kind of drug," the High Wraith rubbed a sore spot on the back of his neck. "He injected me with it, and then left me behind. When I finally came to, you were gone."

"That still doesn't explain how Miller was not himself," Saint pointed out.

"The council had been getting reports from all over Europe that Wraiths were abandoning their posts and joining the ranks of the new vampire lord," Xavier explained. "Whether it was by coercion, or by choice, the council doesn't know. That's why I was assigned to you."

Saint looked at the High Wraith oddly. "Did the council think I would join this new lord as well?"

"They weren't sure," Xavier admitted, "but because of your 'unique' physiology, it couldn't be allowed to happen."

"That's why you were acting so strangely," Saint said, finally catching on. "You wanted to see how I would handle the situation. You wanted to see my true colors, so to speak."

Xavier nodded.

"Why didn't you tell me?"

"What was I supposed to say?" Xavier asked quickly. "Should I have grabbed you and asked, 'Are you a bad guy now?'"

"I see your point."

Xavier smiled softly. He placed a hand on the young woman's shoulder. "Are you okay?"

Saint took a deep breath. "No."

The High Wraith understood. "Anything I can do?"

Saint looked at the hole in the ceiling. "Get me out of here."

***

Pushing her body hard and ignoring the pain searing across the soles of her feet, she glanced over her shoulder nervously as she ran full throttle down the darkened corridors of the academy. Kara slammed her foot against a pile of concrete and crumbled hard to the floor. Skidding to a stop, she rolled quickly onto her back and watched the blood begin to well up from the new scrapes. Ignoring the biting pain in her arms, she lifted herself to her knees and stood up. Looking back into the dimly lit hallway she had just exited, she still saw them: two pairs of golden eyes glowing in the distance. They didn't seem to be closing on her, but they were never out of sight either. They were stalking her.

Turning, she charged into the darkness again. She didn't have time to sneak or hide, only to run as fast as her body would take her. As far as she knew, she was the last living Wraith in the Academy. It was a heavy burden to bear. She had to ensure that someone lived through this ordeal to inform others of what had happened. She felt akin to Paul Revere riding through town shouting at the top of her lungs that "The British are coming, the British are coming!" Weaving in and out of damaged rooms, she tried to lose her stalkers, but the open wounds on her arms and feet made that nearly impossible. The vampires could track the scent of blood in any condition, even through water. It made her erratic escape pattern nearly pointless. Still, it gave her the smallest shred of hope that she could escape. She had to succeed.

Twisting around a damaged wall into an adjoining chamber, Kara stopped and pressed herself against it. Taking deep, quick breaths into her lungs, she tried to catch her breath. Still in shock after seeing Jasmine unceremoniously killed, her body was teetering on the verge of breaking down. Her reserves were gone. She was running on fumes now, but she had to keep going. Leaning her head back for a moment, she lifted her arms and placed her hands on the top of her head. Taking big breaths into her tired lungs, she tried to calm herself for a moment. Her mind started to wander. She couldn't go on like this much longer. The vampires had her beat in every physical category, including stamina. She had to find a place to hunker down, but her bloody wounds made that nearly impossible. There had to—

A pale, clawed hand smashed through the wall next to her and grabbed for her throat. With a shriek, Kara bolted away and took off again into the

Academy.

They were toying with her now. Trying to calm her thumping heart, she glanced nervously over her shoulder as she ran. The ever-present eyes were still there, just watching her from a distance. Turning back around, her eyes widened. Stumbling to a stop, she fell back on her butt. Two men, dressed in tattered clothes with grimy faces, stood silently before her. She knew in that instant, she was dead. With vampires behind her and these two men blocking her progress, there was nowhere to escape. Kara began to panic. Skittering backwards on her hands and pushing with her feet, she tried to get away from the men. Both men reached into their tattered coats and pulled out automatic weapons. Snapping off the safeties and cocking the weapons, the two men extended their arms and brought the weapons to bear on Kara. The first man squeezed the trigger firing off multiple rounds.

Opening her eyes slowly, Kara saw the man fire again. Looking down at her chest, she found no bullet holes or blood. Looking up at the men in confusion, she watched both fire in unison.

The second man, still holding his weapon, reached down with his free hand. "Let me help you," he said with a trace of an odd accent. Kara suddenly recognized it as American.

Tentatively taking the man's hand, she stood up with his help. "Who are you?"

"Stay here," the first man commanded.

Without an answer or any hint of who they were, the two men charged past Kara directly toward the golden eyes in the distance. As they ran, they continued to fire wildly, laying down suppression fire. As they disappeared into the darkness of the Academy, Kara heard a symphony of shrieks, growls, and roaring. Moments later, one of the vampires sailed through the air and landed at her feet. As it cried out and writhed on the floor, she could see four large gashes on its chest that blazed with blue flame. Taking a step back, she watched the creature die as its body was reduced to ash. As the red embers from its body flitted into the air around her, she heard silence once again wash over the Academy.

From the darkness, the two men appeared again. Holstering their weapons back into their jackets, they stopped in front of the young Wraith. The first man extended his hand. His face was a blank slate. "Take my hand if you want to live."

Kara slowly placed her hand in his.

CHAPTER FOURTEEN

Saint, Xavier, and Carl stood silently and surveyed the damage. The stench of smoke and burning bodies was heavy on the air amidst the ruins that used to be the Wraith Academy. Looking into the courtyard, they could see the sky above the village was red as the houses and buildings burned. Apparently, the vampires hadn't stopped with the Academy, but had carried their destruction throughout the entire town. No Wraith lived in the town. Its only crime was housing the facility, and for that, it had paid dearly with the lives of its men, women, and Saint knew, its children.

Huge clouds of black smoke rolled into the sky, blotting out the stars that Saint had first seen. The sound of screams and emergency sirens polluted the air around them. At the massive gates to the Academy, they could see several abandoned emergency vehicles, their red and blue lights still bathing the area. The vampire's destruction of the Wraith Academy was total. Moving slowly through the wreckage, all three realized they had no place to go. The revelation hit them like a ton of bricks. Each lived and worked at the Academy, including Carl. Their home was gone.

"What happened here?" Saint asked slowly.

"I couldn't even hazard a guess," Xavier answered.

Carl looked at the other two with a long face. "I think the question we should be asking is what do we do now?"

Saint and Xavier were silent.

"Shouldn't we track down the bastard responsible for this?" Carl asked angrily, "and extract a little vengeance from his ass?"

"We are only two Wraiths," Xavier said slowly. "We are in no position to retaliate. Plus, we still don't know the identity of this new Vampire Lord."

"Shouldn't be hard to find him," Carl grunted. "Just follow the trail of destruction this guy seems to leave."

"What do you want us to do?" Saint asked angrily. "Should we blaze off into the night to fight and die needlessly? Is that what you want?"

"I don't know," Carl breathed after the reprimand.

"We need to be smart about this," Saint continued. "We can't just go out and start killing every vampire we find. We have to figure out who did this, track him, and then take our revenge. Nothing can be accomplished when you're fighting angry," Saint pointed out. "Vengeance has the nasty habit of getting you killed."

"Saint's right," Xavier confirmed. "Right now, we need to focus on securing the Academy and searching for survivors. That should be our primary goal." The High Wraith stopped as a thought occurred to him. Turning to his left, he stared into the east wing. "Damn."

"What?" Saint asked quickly.

Xavier turned to look at the younger Wraith. All the blood had drained from his face making him look as white as a sheet. "The council."

"We don't know anything," Saint said quickly.

"They could've gotten free."

"Or not," Xavier added. "If they have fallen, we're doomed."

"Why?" Carl asked, obviously not familiar with the inner workings of the Gwyliad Wriaeth. "Why are they so important?"

"They are the Wraith ruling body," Xavier replied. "From this Academy, they coordinate our entire operation. They are the head of our fight against the darkness."

Carl gasped. "Shit. I didn't know this place was that important. Aren't there other councils?"

Xavier nodded. "Yes, but they are merely in place to carry out the instructions of the High Council. They are not ancients, nor are they considered 'true' leaders of the Wraith."

Saint nodded. "If we lose them—"

"I get it," Carl said quickly. "Bad mojo."

"Indeed," Xavier interjected. "The Wraith will fall."

"We need to get to the council chambers," Saint said, moving toward the east wing. "Pronto," she added.

The three moved through the debris and bodies toward the council chambers. Picking up a discarded scythe from the ground, Saint activated the weapon. Holding it tightly in her hand, a sense of doom and foreboding fell over her.

As the three disappeared into the darkness of the Academy, two figures materialized out of the gloom very near where they had just been standing. Their heavy black cloaks wafted around them as they watched the three go.

210

Brigitte pulled back her hood and turned to the other figure. "Is that your quarry, Master?"

Bane watched the young Wraith with burning eyes. "Yes. I must have her."

Brigitte returned her attention to the door the three had just entered. "Why?"

"She possesses a power," Bane boomed, "that I must have. Did you take care of the council?"

Brigitte nodded.

Bane smiled behind his metal mask. "Let them make it to the council chambers and see our work. Then we will take them."

The two vampires melted into the darkness.

***

Saint and Xavier stared into the darkness of the council chambers. The doors had been completely blown from their hinges. Fragments were scattered about the floor, while the two largest chunks lay silently just inside the chamber. No light was visible inside at all. Less than a foot inside the door, the darkness seemed to be thick, like a fog that settled in on the room. There was no way to make out if the council were still in the chamber, or if vampires waited instead. No trace of the columns or raised platform could even be hinted at in the pervasive darkness.

Xavier sniffed the air. Dropping down to his knees, he inspected a dark discoloration on the floor just beyond the darkness. Pressing his fingertip in it, he lifted it to his nose and took another whiff. "Wraith blood," he said slowly. "Old Wraith

211

blood."

Saint's sense of foreboding deepened. Still holding her activated scythe in her right hand, she felt her grip involuntarily tighten. Grabbing the flashlight off her belt, she clicked it on and shone the white light inside. The room appeared to be completely empty. Taking a tentative step beyond the door, she swept the ceiling and walls with the light. Carl and Xavier took up positions on either side of the young Wraith, each activating their own flashlights. They moved carefully into the cavernous room, the two Wraith's senses focusing on every nook and cranny they came across. Saint swept her light up and over the raised platform at the back of the chamber. As she moved quickly, she glimpsed something in the darkness. Slowly pulling her light back, she spotted it again. As she stared at the object, her heart began to throb wildly in her chest. Rushing forward, she vaulted over the massive steps and landed on the platform just in front of the object. Focusing her light down, her fears were realized.

There before her, in a bloodstained white robe, was the body of One. His chest bore large, bloody gashes, and his throat was slit from its collar to just below its chin. Turning away, she looked over the rest of the platform. Huge bloodstains littered the floor as well as a pile of ash in the corner that was previously a vampire. At least they took one of the bastards with them, Saint thought. She turned and started for the stairs. There was nothing here for them. The council was dead, and so was the Gwyliad Wriaeth.

"Emily…"

Saint spun quickly on her heels and looked at One. Dropping down next to the Elder, she grabbed its wrist and placed two fingers over its major artery. There, although almost imperceptible, was a weak heartbeat. She quickly placed her hand on its forehead and stared into its yellow eyes. "Master?"

One's eyes blinked slowly and focused on Saint. "Emily," One said again with a slight smile on its lips. One's voice was weak and barely perceptible. "The rest of the council is dead," it informed her.

Saint held her master's hand, "I know. What can I do?" She turned to see Xavier and Carl moving quickly up the stairs toward them.

"There is little to be done, my child," One said knowingly. "I am dying. I don't think there's anything that can stop my death now."

Saint's face grew long as she placed her hand on the side of One's face. "There has to be a way."

"As Wraiths grow ancient," One said slowly, "our bodies are weakened by the virus. An elder, such as myself, is as fragile as a newborn baby. Our bodies cannot take much stress."

It was another revelation to Saint. It seemed logical that Wraiths would grow more powerful with age, much like vampires, but the opposite seemed to be the case. "I can't let you die," she pleaded.

"Don't worry, child," One said as its irises dilated. "I am in very little pain now. I am ready to pass over."

"Don't say that," Saint pleaded. "You have to

live!"

One's head began to fall back as his eyelids fluttered. "I have...little—" A wave of coughing interrupted his words. Saint watched as blood was forced from his mouth onto his face. A gurgle began to emanate from deep in his throat.

"Master," Saint said, squeezing his hand tightly. "Master?"

Xavier placed his hand on her shoulder. "I think One's gone."

Saint gasped for breath. Everyone who was important in her life had died today. She felt herself begin to hyperventilate as panic set in. Falling forward onto One's chest, she grabbed its robe and pressed it to her face.

"What a touching moment." The three turned to see Bane and Brigitte standing just inside the doorway. "Allow me to introduce myself," Bane said quickly, "I am Lord Bane, and this is my general, Brigitte." The two began to walk confidently into the room.

"It's too bad you couldn't have been here earlier, their blood was exceptional," Brigitte cackled, pointing to the council. "It was aged just perfectly."

Xavier pulled his scythe from his belt and activated it. "You should not be here, vampires."

"You know," Brigitte said with a shrug, "That's the same thing the council said. See where it got them?"

"Silence," Bane commanded. "We are not here to fight."

"That's too bad," Xavier quipped, "Because

214

that's exactly what you're going to get."

Bane waved his hand, dismissing the High Wraith. "We're here for her."

Saint, still kneeling next to One, glanced over her shoulder to see the masked vampire staring at her. Slowly placing One's hand on its chest, she stood and turned to face the two vampires leaving her scythe and flashlight on the floor. "Why me?"

"What is your name?" Bane asked.

Saint looked to her two friends, then back to the vampires. "Emily St. Louise."

"Perfect," Bane cackled. "It's true. The blood of a saint." He looked at Xavier and Carl. "You two do not interest me. If you leave now, I will let you live." He started toward Saint.

Xavier gritted his teeth. "Like hell." Lunging forward, he brought his scythe over his head. Coming down in front of Bane, he brought his weapon down toward the vampire's head. To his surprise, his attack was blocked...by another scythe.

Without even flinching, the Vampire Lord laughed at the High Wraith. "You cannot strike me down."

Xavier followed the shaft of the second scythe down to the porcelain hands of Brigitte standing beside her master. Pulling his weapon free, he took a wary step back. To see a vampire holding a Wraith's weapon was sickening. This was an instrument of good. To see it perverted in the hands of a vampire was an affront to everything he stood for.

"I gave you a chance," Bane rumbled, "but

215

now you must die."

Brigitte pushed past her master and swung her scythe around, nearly connecting with Xavier. Only his quick block saved him. Parrying her move, he spun with his weapon and pressed his attack. Bringing the scythe around his body, he dropped low to hit her legs. As Brigitte leapt up to avoid the blade, she brought her own weapon over her back to counter his next attack. With a grunt and a devious smirk, she pushed his weapon away, brought hers over her head, and swung it down hard. Rolling to his left to avoid the blade, Xavier landed on his back and kicked out Brigitte's legs. As the vampire rolled down the steps, the fight continued.

***

"Emily," Bane said, "you are the chosen one. Your coming has been prophesized by not only the Wraith, but the vampires as well."

Saint kept a healthy distance between her and the hulking Vampire Lord. Over Bane's shoulder, she could see Carl moving toward Xavier's fight. "What are you talking about?"

"You are a new breed," Bane answered. "Neither human, vampire, nor Wraith. You are something different." He reached the top of the steps and stood staring at her, his golden eyes burning behind the mask. "The prophecy says that a saint's blood will create a new race, but it doesn't specify how they will be aligned. Join us, Emily. Together, you and I can rule this pathetic world.

216

We can create an army that will march unheeded across the face of the globe. All will bow before us."

"You're lying. I don't believe you," Saint said, shaking her head.

"I once thought as you did," Bane said after a moment. "I knew the Wraith would vanquish the vampires and free humanity from the unseen darkness that existed just below the surface. That all changed the day the High Council sent me to my death."

"You were a Wraith?"

"Uninitiated," Bane answered, "but still in the Gwyliad Wriaeth's service. Men were needed so desperately for a campaign, they sent my men and I without receiving the ritual. We were mere humans as we faced the onslaught of vampires. All of us died that night, or were turned. They used us," Bane growled. "I only found out later that we were merely a distraction that night. The council was being relocated and they sent all of us to die to distract the vampires."

Saint was speechless.

"Do you still love your precious Wraith now?" Bane asked angrily. "They will use you, as they did me."

Saint thought back to her time in the facility downstairs. They were doing the same thing to her. Testing her, taking her blood, all to find out how to make more of her. Both sides wanted to use her for their own purposes. She looked up at Bane's mask and the sudden realization struck her: it was her fault. The Academy had been obliterated, and the council, Master Quinn, and Miller were dead because of her. It was her fault. Taking an uneasy step back, she couldn't tear her eyes away from Bane's mask.

"Join me," Bane said again as he lifted his hand palm up, "or we will take you by force. The decision is yours."

"I…" Saint's mouth was dry. Glancing to her right, she stared at One's body and her scythe lying next to it. They had all died because of her. Tonight, she had lost her home, her teacher, her best friend, and her creator. In one fell swoop, Bane had taken everything from her. There was nothing left for her now—nothing but the fight. Everything the Wraith had taught her was all she had now. She had to cling to that. Resolved, she knew she could not let their deaths be in vain. No matter what the Wraith did to her, she would not align herself with him. She would not be the cause of any more destruction and death. "I will not join you."

"Very well," Bane said. Holding his arms outside his cloak, he snapped open his arm blades. "Then you must die." He lunged toward her.

Raising her hand, Saint focused all her power into her palm. To her amazement, her scythe leapt up from the floor and shot into her hand. Grabbing the shaft with both hands, she activated the weapon and brought it up in time to block Bane's attack. Snapping the weapon over in her hands, she freed herself and retaliated. As the two slammed their weapons together over and over again, Bane proved to be the dominant fighter of the two. He easily pushed Saint to the back of the platform. Knocking her scythe up, he whipped his blade across her stomach cutting her. As the Wraith tried to retaliate, Bane kicked her hard in the pelvis and knocked her free of the platform. Falling off the back, Saint sailed down toward the floor, but to her surprise, kept falling. Glancing down into the darkness, Bane retracted his arm blades and started down the long stairs. He knew where she was.

***

Xavier brought up his scythe and blocked another of Brigitte's attacks. The two were evenly matched in strength and speed. Gaining the upper hand would be difficult, but not impossible. Pushing the vampire back off the stairs, the High Wraith threw blow after blow trying to break her defenses. As the weapons clacked and clanged together, he felt he was getting the better of her. Bringing his weapon around his body confidently, he lunged again. But his confidence was his undoing. Brigitte countered the attack. Hitting the activation button again, the curved blade of the scythe snapped open. Drawing it quickly back, she caught it just behind his hand. The two combatants' eyes met for a moment. As Xavier's widened, a horrible grin spread across Brigitte's face. With one yank, she pulled her weapon free and excised the Wraith's left hand.

Falling back with a cry of pain, Xavier snapped his hand around the gaping wound and tried to stop the bleeding. Rolling onto his back, he writhed in pain on the floor.

"Pitiful Wraith," Brigitte sneered. Bringing her scythe around, she jabbed the point into his throat. "Now you won't have a date on Friday nights. Are you ready to meet your creator?"

Carl stood on the edge of the platform above Brigitte. Summoning all his courage, he yelled at the top of his lungs and threw himself forward. Throwing his hands forward, he grabbed the vampire and crushed her to the floor. As she stumbled to get up, Carl wrapped his arms around her neck and held on for dear life.

"Get off me!"

Brigitte clawed at Carl, opening huge gashes in his arms and shoulders. Throwing herself forward, she tried to dislodge her passenger. Spinning around, she slammed Carl into the stairs. Pulling back, she hit him again. Carl could feel his ribs cracking under the force of her impacts. Gathering all his strength, he wrapped his arms tighter around her neck. Brigitte had enough.

Leaping straight off the floor, she grabbed onto the ceiling with her claws and clung tightly. "Better hold on, bitch," she sneered. Pulling her claws free, she let go.

***

Saint slowly lifted her head. Pressing her hand to the back of it, she pulled away her fingertips and saw daubs of red blood on them. Cursing under her breath, she sat up, only to have a rush of pain hit her in the head. Gritting her teeth, she fought through the pain and stood up. Scooping her scythe off the floor, she held the deactivated weapon at the ready. Looking straight up, she saw the hole she had fallen through. Roughly rectangular, it was situated directly behind the raised platform. Its purpose was a mystery to Saint.

Lowering her eyes, she glanced around. The area was dark and foreboding. Red lights similar to the ones she had seen in the elevator shaft ran along the edges of the floor and ceiling, casting an ominous glare. This area seemed similar to the research facility she was in earlier, but different. Its very essence seemed to be tainted with darkness. She was standing in a roughly rectangular corridor that seemed to stretch off in both directions as far as her eyes could see. Turning to her left, she began to walk slowly, trying to understand where she was.

There were no doors in the corridor. The walls were completely sheer, except for the repeating presence of seams every five feet. Small grates were situated along the floor and regularly belched out great clouds of steam. The air was thick with moisture and the steam reflected the red lights. Once again, she felt as if she had descended into the very bowels of Hell. Carefully avoiding the grates and searing hot steam, she moved further into the corridor. It seemed to be endless, yet she knew it had to lead somewhere. She had to keep going.

Up ahead, she spotted the end of the corridor. Moving slowly, she stopped at the end and peered out. The area beyond the corridor was a huge, circular chamber, bathed in the same red light. Looking like an amphitheater, the room gradually lowered step-by-step into a huge circle at the bottom. Tall pillars inscribed with another forgotten ancient language ringed the top tier. Taking a step inside, she understood what this place was—another gift from her new genetic memory.

This was the Tribunal. If a Wraith went rogue, or took the life of an innocent human being, he or she was tried before the council and a jury of their peers. The accused would be chained to the floor in the bottom circle while the council and jury sat around them asking questions. If they were found to be guilty, they were executed on the spot. If not, they were freed and allowed to ascend back up into the company of their peers. Many Wraiths had lost their lives in this place. Even now, she could see their anguished faces as they faced their punishment.

Taking a step further into the room, the hair on the back of her neck stood up. Activating her scythe, she saw Bane materialize out of the corner of her eye. Just as he brought his blades down, Saint parried the blow.

"Why do you resist?" Bane asked as their weapons were locked together. "I offer you the chance to rule by my side!"

Saint cocked her head to the right and then to the left, popping her neck. "I will never join you."

Breaking free of the lock, Saint brought her scythe around and sliced through the black cloth of Bane's shirt. Moving back just enough to avoid the enchanted blade, Bane brought his own blades down and knocked her scythe away. Stumbling back as her weapon skittered to the bottom of the Tribunal, Saint moved into a defensive position.

Balling up her fists, she took another step back from Bane, hoping to counter the reach of his weapons. As the big vampire lunged, Saint dodged to avoid the razor-sharp weapons as they cut easily though one of the stone pillars and knocked several large chunks to the ground.

Hitting the edge of the top tier, she lost her balance and tumbled down the steps. Leaping off the top tier with his feet together, Bane glided eerily down toward her. Lifting into a three-point position, Saint shot forward and lowered her shoulder just as Bane landed. Catching the vampire squarely in the chest, she knocked him to the ground. Reeling back, she lifted her hand and called for her scythe again. As the weapon leapt into her hand, she activated it and brought it around just in time to block Bane's next attack.

"Impressive," Bane cackled, "you have controlled your fear." He pulled back his blades and lunged again. "But you still have much to learn."

As their weapons clanked together, Bane pressed his attack, driving her deeper into the Tribunal. Fighting with all her strength and knowledge, Saint knew this vampire easily outclassed her. He was, by far, the superior warrior. Her only hope now was escape.

***

Brigitte and Carl hit the floor with a sickening crunch. The vampire heard the man gasp once as his arms fell free. Standing slowly, she adjusted her cloak and stared down at the human. Lifting her foot, she prepared to bring it down squarely on his skull.

"We're not finished."

Brigitte turned just in time to see a quick flash of steel. Looking up oddly, she saw Xavier standing before her with his scythe in his remaining hand. He looked weak and tired, ready to fall at any moment. Brigitte started to take a step toward him, but felt a line of searing pain across her throat. Lifting her hand, she pressed it to her neck and pulled away a handful of blood. Taking another step, she felt the warmth of her own blood welling up inside her throat. Opening her mouth, the viscous red substance spilled over her lips. Falling to her knees, she saw the first wisps of blue flame flicker up around her head. Looking up at the Wraith in awe, Brigitte fell forward to the ground. As her body hit, her head rolled free of her body.

Dropping the scythe to the floor, Xavier stumbled quickly toward Carl. Dropping down next to him, he placed his only remaining hand on Carl's chest. "Are you alive?"

Carl coughed and sputtered. "Your bedside manner sucks."

Xavier nodded. Looking up at the council chamber doors, he saw three figures standing silhouetted by the light. Letting out a long sigh, he lifted himself from the floor. He didn't have any fight left in him. Grabbing his discarded scythe from the ground, he activated the weapon and readied himself. The three figures walked slowly into the room. As they neared the High Wraith, he recognized them. He quickly snapped the scythe shut and returned it to his belt.

A young girl, maybe twelve or thirteen years of age, rushed across the floor with her arms spread wide. Grabbing onto Xavier, she squeezed him tightly. "I didn't think I would ever see another Wraith again," she admitted. "I'm glad I'm not the only one."

Xavier patted the student Wraith on the back of the head. "It's good to see you too, Kara." He looked up at the two men. "Did the council call for you?"

"No," the first man said, "there was no distress call made."

"We felt the disturbance," the second man admitted. "We came as soon as we understood. Where is the council?"

"Dead," Xavier admitted. "There was a young Wraith with us," he added. "She's fighting the Vampire Lord who did this single-handedly. Carl and I are in no condition to help her."

"We will aid the young Wraith," the first man confirmed. He lifted his head and sniffed the air.

"She went—"

The first man stopped him with a wave of his hand. "We already have her scent." Without another word, the two men shot off toward the platform and leapt fearlessly off the back of it.

Xavier returned his attention to Kara and Carl. "We need to get the two of you away from here. There are still vampires about."

Kara nodded, refusing to let go of the High Wraith.

Leaning down, Xavier lifted Carl from the

225

ground with his good hand. Propping Carl's arm over his and Kara's shoulders, the three started to slowly limp toward the doors.

***

Saint fought hard, but she knew she was losing. Lifting her scythe with both hands, she blocked Bane's attack and parried. Missing her target by a wide margin, she felt her muscles quiver with fatigue. She was quickly running out of steam and Bane showed no signs of stopping. He would wear her down and then move in for the kill. His plan was simple but effective. Ducking below Bane's swipe with his right arm, she rolled backwards and stood up just as the massive vampire attacked again. Bringing his right blade horizontally across her body, Saint blocked the attack with her scythe, but it left her open for his next attack. Bringing his right blade straight up, the tip caught Saint in the cheek and sliced through her flesh.

With a gasp, she stumbled away. She could feel the warm blood running down her cheek from the cut. As she tried to regain her composure, Bane attacked again, this time cutting across her shoulder and her upper thigh. Weak and tired, Saint crumbled to the ground, her body screaming in pain.

The massive vampire stood over her with balled fists and his blades ready for the death stroke. "You should have taken my offer," he boomed. "We could have ruled it all."

"Still not interested," she quipped.

Saint focused all her remaining energy. Lifting her hand, she reached out and grabbed the largest chunk of pillar that Bane had cut free. Closing her eyes, she pulled it toward her with all her strength. The stone only twitched at first, but quickly launched into the air. The chunk sailed through the air, tumbling as it neared. As Bane lifted his arms to strike, the rock slammed into his back and knocked him to the ground. The Vampire Lord's head snapped against the floor with a clang, revealing that his mask was real, not an illusion. Saint quickly lifted herself off the floor and retrieved her scythe. Looking down as the vampire rolled onto his back, she saw that the bottom left section of his mask had been broken off. His flesh beneath was pale gray and littered with scars of every shape and size. Portions of his cheek had completely rotted away with his teeth readily visible. A large gash ran across his cheek and mouth where the mask had cut him. His blood flowed like water from the wound.

Bane clamped his hand over the missing portion of the mask. Roaring at the top of his lungs, he leapt up and faced Saint. "You should not have done that."

Saint's eyes moved up to a dark form in the doorway of the tribunal. She whipped her weapon around her body in a flourish. With a smile, she snapped it shut and took a step back.

"You are unwise to lower your defenses," Bane growled.

Saint shook her head. "I don't think so." She pointed over his shoulder. "The cavalry has arrived."

Bane turned slowly to see two men standing silently in the doorway. His golden eyes hardened as he recognized what they were. He turned back to Saint. "If they attack, I will strike you down."

The sound of guttural growls and moans filled the room.

Saint took a step further away from Bane. "I don't think you'll get the chance."

Bane glanced over his shoulder nervously. The two men were walking into the room while pulling off their tattered clothes. As he tossed his shirt away, the first man dropped to his knees and balled his fists. Snapping his head back, his eyes opened wide exposing the red irises. Opening his mouth wide, large fangs began to grow from the top and bottom rows of his mouth. His face suddenly pulsed and throbbed as his mouth was transformed. Pushing out from his head, it started to take on the shape of a canine muzzle. The second man had dropped to one knee as well. Arching his back, the flesh of his torso ripped open, revealing a thick coat of fur beneath. Grabbing the edges of their flesh with their hands, they began to tear the remainder away exposing more and more fur. Standing up, their knees snapped forward as huge muscles bulged on their thighs and calves. They began to move forward as their transformation neared completion.

A hybrid of wolf and man, the werewolves were perfect engines of destruction. Their fanged mouths dripped with venomous saliva while the six inch claws on the hands and feet were razor sharp. Standing upright like a man, yet slightly hunched at the shoulders, the beasts towered nearly eight feet above the floor and were twice as wide as Bane and Saint combined. The first wolf's coat was a mixture of dark brown and black. He had black fur around his head that ran down his throat and terminated just above his pectoral muscles. The dark fur reappeared just below his elbows and knees. The second man was a mixture of black and silver. Predominantly black, large streaks of silver ran down his chest and his legs. A single stripe of silver fur ran along the crest of his head to the nape of his neck giving him the appearance of a silver mohawk.

Their powerful red gazes scanned over the room and locked onto Bane. Dropping down onto their hands, the mighty animals lunged toward the Vampire Lord and attacked. Bane stumbled back, avoiding the first swipe of their claws, but both were too much for him. Fighting and slicing with his blades, he worked his way back up the Tribunal. Taking a step back, he avoided another swipe from the silver wolf, but the other caught him off-guard, Opening its claws wide, it brought them down and dug deep into the vampire's chest, creating three huge, deep gashes. Grunting, Bane fell back but managed to remain standing. Lunging forward, he embedded both of his blades deep in the chest of the silver wolf. The wolf threw his head back and howled in pain as its blood spurted from the wounds. The black wolf lunged forward and clasped his huge hand around Bane's head. Picking him off the ground, he pulled the vampire's blades free of his companion's chest. In a rage, the wolf summoned all its strength and tossed the vampire across the Tribunal. Bane slammed into the far wall head first and crumbled to the ground.

Slowly picking himself off the floor, Bane snapped his arm blades closed. Blood poured over his silver mask and dripped off the bottom. "You will regret this," he warned. He looked down into the bottom of the Tribunal at Saint. "I will find you again, and next time, you won't have your pets to protect you." Crossing his arms over his chest, he bowed and shimmered from sight. His laughter could be heard echoing throughout the Tribunal as he vanished.

Saint slowly turned to face the two gigantic werewolves standing above her. She saw that the silver wolf had fallen and the black wolf was doing its best to tend to the wounds. Quickly, both creatures reverted to their human forms. The first man quickly began applying pressure to the other's wounds.

Walking up the stairs, Saint looked over the two men. "Is he going to be all right?"

The first man took a breath and nodded after a moment. "His wounds are not fatal. He will heal." The man looked up to Saint. "I am Ben, and this is Creighton."

Saint smiled softly. "Ben. That was my Master's name."

"I'm sorry," Ben replied.

"No," Saint took a breath, "you do the name great justice."

"Help me get Creighton up," Ben asked. "He needs immediate medical attention."

230

Saint nodded. Dropping down, she helped lift Creighton off the ground. Throwing his arms over their shoulders, they lifted his legs and carried him out of the Tribunal.

CHAPTER FIFTEEN

Three days had passed since the attack on the Academy. Saint and Ben had returned the morning after in broad daylight to round up the last remaining Wraiths who were either hidden or pinned inside. All told, the death toll was just shy of five hundred. Less than one hundred Wraiths, students, and support staff made it out alive. Bane's attack had been utterly devastating and had crippled the Gwyliad Wriaeth. The High Council, and most of the oldest Master Wraiths, including Ben Quinn, were dead. There were other academies with other councils, but without a central ruling body, the Wraith teetered on the brink of chaos. News had reached the far corners of the Vampire Lord Bane's triumph over the Wraith and even as the moments ticked by, other vampires emerged from the darkness to try and take a shot at them. They were no longer the invulnerable hunters. Life would never be the same again.

Saint sat at a small table in a yellow and blue painted kitchen. Large, white bandages clung to her face and peeked out above her tank top. Setting the butcher's knife on the table, she sat back and admired her work for the first time. She had gone with a traditional design this year. It just felt right. Placing her hands on the sides of the large, orange pumpkin in front of her, she turned it and admired the face she had carved. Two large triangular eyes stared out at her above a jagged-toothed smile.

Grabbing a small candle and a book of matches from the side of the table, she lit it and placed it carefully inside the jack-o-lantern. Lifting the cap from the discarded innards, she placed it carefully on top and turned it until it fell into place. Standing up from the table, she wiped of bit of excess pumpkin guts from her shirt and pants. Walking across the kitchen, she killed the lights and returned to stare at her creation. As the candle flickered inside, she smiled. It's perfect, she thought.

Ben stood in the doorway of the kitchen staring at the Wraith. "Happy Halloween."

Saint looked up with the smile still on her face. "Happy Halloween," she echoed.

Ben had been nice enough to let her stay at his home until she could find her own. His tiny, one-bedroom, one-bathroom cottage wasn't much, but at least it had a couch she could crash on. And Ben's cooking wasn't that bad either. Plus, it was only fifteen minutes walking time from London if she needed an escape. She hadn't needed it…just yet.

"How are you feeling?" Ben asked, leaning against the doorframe.

Saint nodded. "I've been better, but I'm okay. My cuts have almost healed." She pulled away the edge of the bandage on her face revealing the small pink scar beneath. "It should be completely gone soon," she said pleasantly.

The two stood in the darkness silently, the glow of the jack-o-lantern illuminating them.

"Any word on Creighton?" Saint asked after a moment.

"He'll be fine. He's with the rest of the pack now," Ben answered. "They will tend to his wounds."

The two fell into a silence again. It wasn't uncomfortable, but not quite familiar yet. They had only known each other for three days, and neither had spoken of that night yet. Either it hadn't come up, or Saint avoided it. Ben was genuinely worried about her. She seemed to be bottling all the loss and pain up inside her. He knew that wasn't healthy.

"So," Ben breathed.

"So," Saint repeated. "How was work?"

Ben shrugged. "Have a 'vette down at the shop that I just can't seem to get running smoothly. It could be the carburetor, or the fuel injection system. Just can't pin it down."

Saint found the idea of a werewolf who was a mechanic by day somewhat strange. All day long, he was up to his elbows in cars and grease, then spent his nights as a preternatural creature who hunted the streets of London. That could be a movie, Saint thought with a smirk. "I know I say this every day, but I really appreciate you letting me stay here."

Ben waved off the comment. "You don't have to keep thanking me. It's the least I could do."

Saint pulled out her chair and slowly slumped into it. Staring at the jagged face of her pumpkin, she placed her elbows on the table and rested her head in her hands. This was the first Halloween she had spent without Miller and Master Quinn in a long time. This had been their favorite holiday. It was the one night of the year that they could walk around in plain sight in full Wraith regalia without even getting a second glance. Saint had even received a compliment on her "costume" last year when she and Miller had attended a local costume party.

She slowly looked up to Ben. "I need to go to work."

Ben nodded. "I know. Need some company?"

Saint shook her head. "Not tonight." Standing up, Saint walked out of the kitchen into the tiny living room. Still wearing the chunky boots she had grabbed three days ago, she had finally removed the dirty, bloody scrubs she had been wearing and destroyed them. Now clad in black slacks and a black tank top, she grabbed her black leather coat off the couch and pulled it on. Pulling her scythe from her pocket, she fastened it to the back of her pants. Moving to the door, she twisted the handle and pulled it open. A burst of cold air whipped around her body as she took a step outside.

"You know where I am if you need me," Ben said slowly.

Saint glanced over her shoulder with a nod. "Thank you." Pulling the door shut behind her, she left Ben with her freshly carved jack-o-lantern.

Looking at the ghoulish smile that Saint had carved, Ben smiled. Leaning over, he blew out the candle and wandered into the living room. It was time for him to go to work as well. Peeling off his clothes, he dropped down to his knees. As his head snapped back, he howled.

***

Wrapping her coat tightly around her body, she

stuffed her hands into her pockets. Lowering her head, she followed a small, well-worn trail that led away from Ben's home. Glancing over her shoulder, she could see the lights of the city. It's where she needed to be, but not where she was going. Turning her gaze to the sky, she felt the cool night air whip through her dark hair. Every single star in the sky seemed to be visible tonight. Staring into the center of them, she looked at the bridge of stars that swept across the sky and formed the Milky Way Galaxy. She had been taught once that there were more stars in the night sky than grains of salt on all the Earth's beaches and deserts combined. Tonight, she believed it. Two of the brightest stars, which she assumed were planets—but she didn't have a strong grasp of astronomy—seemed to be watching over her as she walked. She named them Miller and Master Quinn, and then chose a third for herself. In that moment, she saw that no matter where they were now, everything was connected. She found a bit of peace in the thought.

Turning off the path, she knew where she was going, but didn't want to admit it to herself. She stared at her feet, but knew the way by heart. She had walked this way a dozen times since arriving here. It had almost become second nature to her at this point. Looking up, she saw a small hill ahead of her. Stopping just short of it, she closed her eyes for a moment and took a deep breath. Each time she came here, it only got harder. Each night she arrived, she wanted to find some kind of peace, some kind of understanding, but the scars on her heart only seemed to deepen at the sight. She wondered for a moment if it was even healthy to be here.

Walking slowly up the hill, she spotted a tree at the top. It was her tree. A massive willow tree, its branches drooped down with age and created a natural canopy against the elements. Reaching the top, she turned and leaned against the mighty trunk and stared off into the distance. This hill was actually part of a much larger range that sloped down and ran off into the distance. From here, she could look across England's rolling hills and grassy plains. In the distance, she could see several small houses and cottages with lit windows and thin wisps of smoke rolling up from their chimneys. Lowering her eyes, she turned, almost hesitantly, toward the two small crosses that had been placed in the ground next to the tree.

Each cross was nothing more than two sticks lashed together with a bit of twine. Without the bodies for a proper burial, she had instead opted to make Miller's and Master Quinn's graves here. She thought they would appreciate the view as she did. Sliding down the tree trunk, she sat down on the cold ground and pulled her knees into her chest. Resting her chin on her kneecaps, she stared at the two grave markers. She never spoke, only listened, hoping to hear their voices, or some sign that they were okay and in a better place. She had, as of yet, heard nothing.

Wrapping her arms around her legs, the events that led her here began to run through her head. Swirling in a mist of emotion, she saw images of the ritual and her final test, and her joy at telling her Master the good news. Flashes of her last night with Miller swam around her mind mingled with the dark form of Bane leering over her. She saw the two werewolves, and the haunting image of Mark's eyes wide open as he lay dead with bite marks in his throat. The ordeal had hardened her in some ways, and scarred her in others. It had taken away everything she held dear, and yet, gave her a new insight into life.

"For each beginning, there is an end," she heard Master Quinn's voice remind her, "And for each ending, there is a beginning."

It was a lesson he had tried to teach her many times. It was only now that she truly understood what he meant. Letting her head fall back against the tree trunk, she stretched out her legs and took in a deep breath. Glancing up at the stars once again, she felt alive for the very first time in her life.

One Destiny…

It will not be easy.

It will be a life without reward, without remorse, without regret.

This path is placed before you, stretching out endlessly into the horizon. The road forks and winds into countless millions of different possibilities, each changing everything. But the path is yours alone.

It will not be easy.

But you will find out who you are.

THE END

238